"How do you do it?" Gary asked.

"Do what?"

Sophie had regained control of her emotionally guarded expression, and he scowled as he walked toward her, stopping mere inches from where she stood.

Gary pointed to her face. Her eyes narrowed. "That. How do you act like you don't care when I know deep down you do? Are you afraid someone will glimpse the real you?"

Sophie shrugged. "What if this is the real me?"

The move ignited the frustration that had been simmering deep inside Gary's gut. He brought his mouth down over hers. Sophie stiffened, but he pinned her to him.

When her lips softened beneath his and her body relaxed, he broke away and headed to the driver's side, all the while ignoring how right it had felt to hold her again.

Sophie still stood where he'd left her, but turned slowly to face him, daggers firing from her dark brown gaze. "What the hell was that?"

"Just wanted to see what it would take to make that control of yours slip. I'd say mission accomplished."

KATHLEEN LONG

WITHOUT A DOUBT

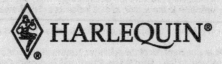

HARLEQUIN®

TORONTO • NEW YORK • LONDON
AMSTERDAM • PARIS • SYDNEY • HAMBURG
STOCKHOLM • ATHENS • TOKYO • MILAN • MADRID
PRAGUE • WARSAW • BUDAPEST • AUCKLAND

ISBN-13: 978-0-373-88715-6
ISBN-10:   0-373-88715-9

WITHOUT A DOUBT

www.eHarlequin.com

Printed in U.S.A.

ABOUT THE AUTHOR

After a career spent spinning words for clients ranging from corporate CEOs to talking fruits and vegetables, Kathleen Long now finds great joy spinning a world of fictional characters, places and plots. She shares her life with her husband and their neurotic Sheltie, dividing her time between suburban Philadelphia and the New Jersey seashore, where she can often be found—hands on keyboard, bare toes in the sand—spinning tales. After all, life doesn't get much better than that. Please visit www.kathleenlong.com for the latest contests, appearances and upcoming releases.

Books by Kathleen Long

HARLEQUIN INTRIGUE
847—SILENT WARNING
914—WHEN A STRANGER CALLS
941—WITHOUT A DOUBT

CAST OF CHARACTERS

Sophie Markham—When she spots a child who bears an uncanny resemblance to her deceased niece, she'll stop at nothing to find out if the child might have survived, even if that means taking advantage of a former love.

Gary Barksdale—When Sophie Markham raises questions about his niece's true identity, he'll do whatever it takes to protect his family, even if that means going toe-to-toe with the woman he once thought he'd marry.

Ally Alexander—The adopted daughter of Maggie and Robert Alexander, and Gary's niece, she's the apple of her family's eye. She's also the spitting image of Sophie's deceased niece. Is the likeness a coincidence, or much more?

Maggie Alexander—After SIDS claimed the life of her only child, she pursued every avenue to have a second child. But how far did she go to make her dream come true?

Robert Alexander—When he facilitated Ally's adoption years before, did he follow the letter of the law? Or did he break the rules to provide his heartbroken wife with another child?

Trevor James—He's become a legend in Philadelphia for providing life and career counseling to the rich and famous. Is he merely Maggie Alexander's life coach, or does his influence go far deeper?

Rebecca Markham—Sophie's sister died too young, after smoking in bed. Was her death a senseless tragedy or something far more sinister? Something no one ever suspected…until now.

Robin Markham—She was Rebecca's infant daughter and Sophie's beloved niece. Did she perish in the tragic house fire along with her mother as investigators claim?

Chapter One

Sophie Markham stood in the middle of the Hilton's ballroom and stared into her past.

Looking at the child was like looking at a ghost—a vision of the young girl her sister had once been, many years before she'd perished in a senseless house fire.

Smoking in bed. Sophie blinked and shook her head. What a waste. She eyed the young girl again, watched how she interacted with her mother, the fund-raiser's organizer.

If Rebecca's infant daughter had survived the fire, she'd be about the same age. Five, Sophie guessed, though goodness knew she had so little experience with kids she wasn't terribly gifted at guessing their age.

"Live in three, Sophie." John Cook,

WNJZ's cameraman, spoke from just behind her left ear.

"Thanks." Sophie wrenched her attention away from the young girl, smoothed the front of her designer suit and smiled at the camera. "Look okay?"

"Gorgeous as always."

"I'm telling you, Cookie, if only you weren't married."

Cook, who was old enough to be her father, shot her a wink then tipped his head toward the event's organizer, Maggie Alexander. "We'd better get set up."

As Sophie crossed the room to where the girl's mother stood, she couldn't keep her focus away from the little girl. When the child's gaze locked with hers, Sophie's breath caught in her throat.

The little girl had the same chestnut-brown hair Becca had as a child, the same button nose. Sophie smiled at the way the girl's pixie haircut framed her curious expression.

"Ally, Mommy's got to talk to Ms. Markham now, so you'll be a good girl, right?"

The child's face softened into a huge grin revealing a wonderfully toothy smile, but as

Ally turned to give her mother a quick nod, it was something entirely different that captured Sophie's attention. It was a birthmark on the back of the girl's neck in the shape of a perfect butterfly. A birthmark identical to the one Sophie's niece, Robin, had been born with.

Sophie blinked, disbelief rushing through her. She never thought she'd see anything like the mark again.

Like a cruel glimpse into the past, the patch of discolored skin brought back memories of the night Becca and Robin had perished. What were the odds two children would have identical birthmarks? Apparently not as high as she might think, because there Ally Alexander stood, bearing Robin's butterfly.

Robin. Who would have been the same age.

A wave of grief threatened to overtake Sophie's emotions, but she shoved it away. Now wasn't the time to let the past get the best of her.

"Sophie." Cookie squeezed her elbow. "Thirty seconds. You all right?"

Sophie swallowed away the tightness in her throat and pasted on a smile, her expression nothing more than a reflex at this stage in her career. She compartmentalized the old grief, locking it inside the back of her brain as Cookie counted down on his fingers. Five. Four. Three. Two. One.

"Sudden infant death syndrome," Sophie began. "It takes the lives of 3,000 children in this country every year and yet it cannot be prevented or predicted.

"With me tonight is Maggie Alexander, chairperson of this year's SIDS gala. Tonight's carnival seeks to raise funds for local organizations that provide support services for area families who have suffered a loss. Organizers hope to spread awareness of the steps you can take to help reduce the risk of SIDS."

She turned her cheek to the camera and gave Maggie a generous smile, hoping the woman would sound as competent and articulate in the interview as she had during their initial conversation. "Mrs. Alexander, this year's attendance seems better than ever. Can you tell me a little bit about how tonight's event can help our community?"

Maggie Alexander proceeded to concisely deliver what Sophie was certain must be a series of practiced talking points. The woman was effective in her comments and kept her tone conversational, without the visible nerves so many interviewees suffered as soon as Cookie turned on the camera light.

"Mrs. Alexander?"

"Please, call me Maggie."

Sophie nodded and let her expression grow serious. "Maggie. If it's not too personal, might I ask how you came to be involved with the program?"

Even though they'd discussed the question beforehand and Sophie knew Maggie was prepared for it, she felt like a heel invading the woman's personal pain for the benefit of a story.

A shadow passed across Maggie Alexander's face as she visibly swallowed. "Of course. Like so many of us active in raising funds and awareness to fight SIDS, my husband, Robert, and I lost a child. Our son." She shot a knowing glance to where her husband stood holding Ally.

"I'm so sorry."

Maggie forced a weak smile. "Thank you."

Sophie reached out and gently placed her

hand against the woman's arm. "Thank you for caring enough to take action. You have my sympathy and my respect."

She turned back to the camera. "And with the help of those in attendance tonight and our viewers at home, together we can work to better understand SIDS."

Cookie extinguished the camera light and headed for his bag of gear.

Mrs. Alexander's throat worked, and Sophie regretted opening the wound of the woman's personal pain. After they said their goodbyes, Sophie turned to the door where Cookie stood waiting.

That's when she saw *him*.

Another vision from her past. This one taller, darker, definitely male.

She hadn't seen Gary Barksdale in seven years, yet the sight of him affected her senses much now as it had the first time she'd set eyes on him.

She'd been a junior at the University of Delaware, testing the waters at a tailgate party before a home football game. She'd always kept to herself, and the party had been a huge step out of her comfort zone.

Sophie remembered thinking she couldn't decide whether her inability to breathe had been due to Gary, or due to some sort of antisocial panic attack.

Based on the current tightness in her chest, she'd put her money on Gary.

Gary Barksdale.

As if one ghost hadn't been enough for the night.

He visibly flinched when he realized she'd spotted him watching her.

Their relationship had been brief but intense—overwhelming both of them with emotions too strong for a pair of college juniors. Sophie had broken things off when she'd realized she'd grown to need and want Gary's presence. Of course, the fact he'd proposed had played a small role in the speed of her departure.

Sophie had once vowed never to need a man after watching her mother's parade of losers. As much as she'd cared for Gary, she couldn't afford to let him past her defenses then—or now.

He looked more solid than she remembered, not in the sense of physique, but in terms of his presence. He'd visibly matured, soft lines edging the corners of his mouth and the patch of skin between his brows, as if he'd spent too much time frowning.

The old, familiar flicker of attraction edged through her, causing her to fake a cough and momentarily glance away. The last thing she needed was for Gary to know she'd never quite gotten over him.

When she recovered from the shock of seeing him, Sophie closed the gap between them, ignoring the tiny voice that told her to run—as fast as she could—in the opposite direction. Seeing Gary was just what her emotions didn't need on top of the memories of Becca and Robin.

The crooked grin she'd once dreamed about slid across Gary's lips, dimpling one cheek.

"Sophie Markham."

The rough notes of his voice sent a shiver up the back of her neck. Damn. After all these years, her nerve endings still snapped to attention at the sound of his voice.

"What brings you here?" One dark blond brow lifted.

Sophie narrowed her gaze. "Working."

His grin spread into what appeared to be a sincere smile. "Kind of figured that out by the television camera and the microphone." He tipped his chin toward her cobalt-blue suit. "Not to mention the getup. Far cry from those sweats you lived in at U of D."

The heat of a blush fired in Sophie's cheeks, and she turned away as if admiring the crowd. "Guess your investigative skills are sharp as always."

"Apparently so."

"Still with the *Inquirer?*" *As if she didn't know.* She turned back to face him now that her warm embarrassment had left her face.

He nodded. "Thinking about making a move, actually."

Sophie widened her eyes, asking the question silently.

"Los Angeles." Gary shrugged. "I'd rather not jinx it by talking about it."

"I never knew you were superstitious."

His only response was a deepening of his tantalizing grin.

Sophie's stomach clenched, but she ignored it. If Gary had plans to relocate cross-country, that gave her all the more reason to ignore any attraction that still lingered between them after all this time.

She redirected the conversation—and her thoughts—to work. Work was safe. Chit-chat was not.

"So what brings the award-winning Gary Barksdale to a fund-raiser for SIDS?"

The words had no sooner left her lips than she wondered whether or not he'd lost a child. Good heavens. It had been so long since she'd seen him, he was probably married with a house full of kids by now. Some people actually developed lives after college.

Sophie wasn't one of them. She'd developed one hell of a career, deciding the corporate fast track suited her much better than thoughts of family, or love.

Gary opened his mouth to answer her question, but Sophie interrupted. "I shouldn't have asked that. I know a lot of attendees have lost a child. You don't have to answer me."

"No children." Gary shook his head. "No wife."

A traitorous note of relief whispered through Sophie's veins, and she mentally chastised herself.

The decision to break off their relationship had been hers. She had no right to feel comforted by the fact he apparently hadn't found anyone to take her place—yet.

"It was my nephew." Gary let out a quick sigh. "Six years ago. Just about devastated our family."

His words jolted her from her selfish thoughts.

His nephew.

Sophie reached out to touch his arm, but withdrew her fingers at the last moment. "I'm so sorry."

"Thanks." He forced a smile that didn't come anywhere close to reaching his eyes. "They say time heals, but I don't think it ever does."

"Do they have other children?" Sophie hated the thought of anyone losing a child, remembering the way the death of her niece had sliced her clean through. She couldn't imagine how a parent would survive.

Gary nodded. "They didn't then. Adam was their one and only. It took them a while to have him. After he died, they tried again, and then chose adoption." He tipped his head across the room. "I don't know where my sister would be today without her."

Sophie followed his gaze to where Maggie Alexander and her daughter stood. Her heart caught.

"Maggie's your sister?"

"If you hadn't dumped me so fast in school, you might have met my family."

Sophie knew she should respond to Gary's dig, but she couldn't convince her brain to focus on anything but the young girl standing across the room, clinging to her mother's hand.

Ally Alexander.

Adopted.

Ally Alexander.

With a birthmark identical to her niece's.

Was there a chance—any chance at all— that Robin had survived the fire? After all, the investigators had found no remains.

What if the little girl the Alexanders had adopted was Robin? Could it be possible?

No.

She was thinking crazy thoughts. If Robin had survived, Sophie would be raising her now. After all, she'd been named guardian by Becca the day Robin was born.

They'd never found any bones that had been identified as Robin's. They'd blamed it on her young age and the intense heat of the fire that had burned out of control for over forty-five minutes.

"Soph? You okay?"

The old nickname jerked Sophie's stare away from Ally Alexander and back to Gary.

A frown had replaced his grin.

Sophie gave a quick shake of her head. "I'm fine. I was just thinking what a lovely family they make."

Gary reached out and wrapped his fingers around her elbow. Heat seared from the point of contact through the thick weave of her suit. "I was sorry to hear about your sister and your niece. I should have called."

Sophie swallowed and shook her head, taking a backward step to free her arm from his touch. "It's okay. Listen, I need to get going." She nodded to where Cookie stood waiting for her at the exit door. "It was good to see you."

"You, too." Gary held out a hand and she shook it, extracting her fingers from his as quickly as she could.

"See you around."

Sophie beat a path across the room and past Cookie, holding her breath until she exited into the cool October air.

"You look like you just saw a ghost," Cookie said as he loaded his equipment into the station's van.

Sophie reached for the passenger door and shot a glance back at the banquet room door. "Call me crazy, Cook, but I think I just saw two."

SOPHIE MARKHAM.

Gary's gut did a sideways roll as he watched the dark-haired beauty walk away. Seven years. Seven years and she still had the same effect on him she'd had when he'd first spotted her on the University of Delaware campus.

His thoughts quickly shifted from the first time he'd seen Sophie to the last. The day she'd walked out of his life with no explanation other than the fact she didn't need a man.

Didn't want a man.

Didn't want *him*.

The warmth that had spread inside his

chest as they'd spoken wavered, cooling to an icy chill.

He'd known their paths would cross at some point. How could they not? He wrote for the largest paper in Philadelphia and Sophie reported for the most popular station. Matter of fact, it was a miracle they hadn't bumped into each other before.

"Uncle Gary!"

The shrill little voice cut through his thoughts and he turned to find his niece, Ally, racing toward him, her patent-leather shoes slapping against the ballroom floor.

He dropped to one knee and braced himself for impact. Ally did not disappoint, launching herself at him as her uninhibited giggle filled the air.

Gary caught her under the arms, giving her a quick squeeze then lifting her up off the floor. He planted a kiss against her rosy cheek. "What's up, kiddo?"

All thoughts of Sophie Markham faded as he took in Ally's toothy grin and the sprinkle of freckles that spread across her pert nose.

"Mommy's giving a party." She nodded, excitement pouring off her small frame.

"And did you see the TV camera? Mommy's famous."

"Yes, she is."

Gary surveyed the room. How his sister had managed to turn the banquet hall into what appeared to be a mini-carnival, he had no idea. Maggie always had been a genius at whatever she put her mind to, and once she'd devoted herself to raising money and awareness for SIDS research, she'd never looked back.

"There she is." Ally pointed to where her mother stood, mixing and mingling like a pro. "Mommy!"

Ally's voice rang out across the room and Maggie's face instantly lit from within as her gaze settled on her daughter. As Maggie closed the gap between them, Gary realized, not for the first time, that he'd do anything to preserve the look of pure joy that painted his sister's features whenever she looked at her daughter.

To say adopting Ally had saved Maggie's life would be an understatement—at least as far as Gary was concerned. He'd feared for his sister during the terrible time after she'd found her son, Adam, dead in his crib. When sudden infant death syndrome had taken his nephew, it had also taken a very big piece of his sister and her husband, Robert.

Their unsuccessful attempts at pregnancy—including financially and physically exhausting fertility treatments—had wrung the couple emotionally dry.

Ally wiggled in Gary's arms as her mother neared, and he lowered her to the floor. She took off like a shot, straight for Maggie.

Gary's gaze fell to the small birthmark that couldn't be a more perfect symbol of what Ally meant to all of them. A butterfly. A tiny, perfect, life-affirming butterfly.

The day she'd floated into their lives, Ally had saved each of them. She'd reawakened the light in his sister's beautiful eyes—the eyes that measured him now.

"Saw you talking to Sophie Markham." Maggie waggled her brows teasingly, her smooth blond hair swinging against her jawline as she tipped her chin. "She's very pretty. And smart. Not sure you're man enough for her."

That, he already knew.

Gary forced a weak smile. "Been there. Done that."

Maggie's brows snapped together and she frowned. "When?"

"College."

"How long?"

He shrugged. "A few months."

Her pale gaze widened. "Serious?"

He shook his head. "Apparently not as far as she was concerned."

They'd grown adept at the art of concise conversations ever since Ally had become a parrot, repeating the last words of most every sentence she heard.

"Serious?" she mimicked her mother now, who gave her a quick squeeze.

Silence beat between Gary and his sister for a moment, then Maggie smiled.

"Well, I thought the woman had it all going on, but she's obviously an idiot."

"Idiot," Ally repeated.

Maggie cringed.

"Thanks, sis." Gary stepped close to his sister and dropped a kiss to her cheek. "Trust me, it's ancient history. Are you going to feed me or what?"

She shifted Ally to one hip and linked her arm through Gary's. "Right this way, handsome."

As they crossed to the spread of appetizers and desserts, Gary fought to center his attention on the two women who loved him—the one at his side and the mini-woman she cradled in her arms.

If he took the Los Angeles job, these two would be what he'd miss most. Any time he seriously considered the position, it was the thought of leaving his family that made him hesitate.

Sophie Markham, on the other hand, would be someone he'd gladly leave behind. Her image flickered across his mind's eye, and his tightening gut belied his tough thoughts.

Sophie Markham—the one woman who had made it quite clear years before that *she* did not love him, nor would she ever.

He worked to shove her image away, but his efforts were futile.

Seeing Sophie tonight had done nothing but sharpen the image that had never been far from Gary's mind since he'd seen her last.

Ancient history?

Not so far as his heart—and pride—were concerned.

But there was no need for anyone but him to ever know the truth.

SOPHIE RUFFLED THE LAYERS of her short hair and braced herself, flipping open the cover of the folder she'd filed away five years ago.

Immediately after Becca and Robin's deaths, she'd pored over every news article that mentioned the fire. She'd hounded the local police and fire departments. She'd been a woman obsessed, dumbstruck by grief and emotional loss.

She drew in a deep breath and held it, unsure whether she was ready to open the door to that pain again.

Careless Smoking Claims Life of Mother and Infant Daughter.

The words cut through her cleaner than any knife ever could. Sophie squeezed her eyes shut, then forced them open, willing herself to revisit that horrible night. Willing herself to reread every single word. Every note she'd made from her interviews of those at the scene.

Every word.

Somewhere here there might be a clue, might be something she'd missed. She couldn't afford *not* to open herself to the old pain.

For five years, she'd accepted her sister and niece were gone. She'd accepted she was now alone, the last living Markham of her family tree. She'd given Becca and Robin a joint funeral befitting royalty, even though Robin's casket had been empty.

The investigators had explained a fire as intense and long-burning as the one that had destroyed Becca's home could have easily destroyed a baby's body and bones. But what if someone had saved Robin from the flames?

What if?

The image of Ally Alexander's unique birthmark flashed through Sophie's mind, and she scrambled for the album she kept safely tucked in her nightstand drawer. Robin's baby album.

She lifted the small object from the drawer, tracing a finger across the yellow duck that graced the cover. Sophie cracked open the treasured collection of snapshots and smiled down at the luminous face that met her gaze.

The navy-blue eyes. The dark brown hair. The pert little nose.

Her throat tightened as she flipped through the images of her niece until she found what she'd been searching for. The close-up of Robin's birthmark.

A perfect butterfly.

Sophie inhaled sharply, squinting at the photo.

Could two children possibly have such an identical mark? Of course, it *might* be possible. But Ally Alexander not only had the identical mark, she also had the same coloring and was similar in age to what Robin would be were she alive.

And she'd been adopted.

Was it possible?

Sophie swallowed hard, thinking of the series of articles Gary Barksdale had written for the *Philadelphia Inquirer* on the kidnapping and recovery of a local girl. The child had been six months old when she'd been kidnapped and four years old when she'd been reunited with her family.

He'd be the perfect person to help her sort through her suspicions and questions about identification, aside from the fact she'd be talking about his cherished niece.

Anxiety battled for its place among the tangle of emotions in her gut.

Gary Barksdale.

Seeing him tonight had been a reality check.

Since they'd split up, she'd worked with a vengeance, first at graduating college with top honors, then at landing a job with WNJZ.

She'd allowed herself to feel the pain, the joys and the triumphs of the stories she covered, yet she'd never let herself become close to anyone after her sister's death.

Not a coworker. Not a friend. Not a lover.

Thoughts of the brief romance she'd shared with Gary rushed into her brain and she warmed instinctively. Her involvement with him had been heady, wonderful and foolish.

Breaking it off had been the smartest move she'd ever made. Watching her sister's abusive relationship a short while later had convinced her she'd made the right move.

Once Robin had been born, Becca had wisely kicked out the man she'd been involved with—Robin's father. He'd threatened violence on more than one occasion and after Becca had filed a restraining order—at Sophie's urging—he'd thankfully disappeared from their lives.

Becca had moved back to the Philadelphia region, ready to make a fresh start with her gorgeous daughter. Sophie had been ready to do whatever her sister and niece needed. Anything.

Tears swam in her vision and she blinked them away.

Anything.

Then everything had changed, and the sister and niece who were her world were gone. Forever.

Or so she'd thought.

She might be grasping at the longest shot of her life, but she had to see it through. She owed that much to her sister's memory.

Her reporter's instinct wouldn't rest until she fully explored the possibilities, and as much as she didn't want to face the man again, she knew exactly where to start.

Chapter Two

Gary pulled open the door to the diner, pausing for a beat to gather himself. He'd been pushing an afternoon deadline when Sophie called. He'd asked her to give him an hour to finish up. He should have asked for two. Maybe then he could have cleaned up a bit.

He ran a hand up through his close-cropped hair then down over the stubble on his jaw, catching himself in the move.

So what if he looked as if he hadn't slept at all last night? He hadn't. The news came first. Sophie knew that. Hell, she lived the life as much as he did, only she had to do it live in front of millions of viewers.

She waved from a booth along the far wall of the quaint room and Gary couldn't help but notice how slender she'd become—not that she'd ever been heavy—but back in the day, the woman had had curves. Serious curves.

He grinned to himself as he crossed the worn linoleum floor, picturing her long brown ponytail shoved up into a baseball cap, her U of D jersey tucked into a pair of tattered jeans, white high-top sneakers on her feet.

What a sight she'd been back then.

Sophie stood and extended her hand.

What a sight she was now.

Gary bypassed the handshake and pressed a quick kiss to her cheek. She blinked and a flush of color spread up her face.

She glanced down at the table, apparently waiting for him to slide into his side of the booth. Her close-cropped, dark hair feathered impeccably around the sharp angles of her cheekbones. Small diamond studs sparkled from each earlobe.

Her crisp white blouse looked as though it had been made for her, the seams perfectly hugging her slender shoulders, the sleeves falling smoothly to the shirt's precise cuffs. A rich brown jacket lay folded on the bench seat next to her, a perfect match for the slim, classic skirt that sheathed her lean hips and thighs.

"I guess you're wondering why I called." Sophie's voice cut through the visual inventory Gary had been taking.

He nodded. She was absolutely right. He was wondering why she'd called. Certainly it hadn't been for old time's sake.

Gary knew she had no interest in picking up where they'd left off seven years earlier. She'd made her feelings crystal clear when they'd parted ways, and Gary had no desire to set himself up for that kind of hurt again. Ever.

He inhaled deeply, shoving the old disappointment out of his head. He'd truly loved her back then, but her heart had been cold and sharp-edged when she'd walked away—as cold and sharp-edged as the rest of her body appeared now.

Maybe she'd done him a favor way back when. Since their breakup, he'd avoided personal entanglements, focusing on honing his reporting skills. His stories had progressively grown bigger and broader, and now he'd attracted the interest of the L.A. paper.

Not bad.

Gary dropped onto the bench seat and Sophie mirrored the move.

"What's up?" he asked, realizing he'd taken far too long to speak.

Her throat worked, and she stared at him as if studying every line and shadow of his face. "It's been a long time."

Her voice was soft, bringing memories of the tender times they'd shared rushing back.

Gary nodded, but kept his features expressionless. "You've certainly changed."

Her solemn features broke into a smile, and for an instant he flashed back on the younger, softer Sophie.

The skin around her eyes crinkled. "Can't say the same for you."

He glanced down at the creases in his denim shirt and the coffee stain on his rolled-up sleeve. He met her gaze and arched his brows, rubbing a hand across his day-old beard. "We don't all have to be live at five."

"I guess we don't," she said softly.

"Speaking of which—" Gary took a long sip of the coffee the waitress had poured into his cup "—don't you have a broadcast to get ready for?"

Sophie nodded, then splayed her hands on the glass tabletop. "I've got a little time first.

How about you?" She lifted her gaze to his. "Can you give me a half hour or so?"

He could. The question was whether or not he wanted to. "Sure," he answered, wondering what the woman was up to.

"I wanted to talk to you about the Hernandez story."

Even though he'd mulled over the possible reasons she might want to see him since her call, it was safe to say the Hernandez case hadn't appeared anywhere on his mental list.

He narrowed his gaze, his curiosity beginning to percolate. "Go on."

"How did they work the identification?"

It was a simple question. Too simple for someone like Sophie. She knew the ropes. Hell, she'd covered the story. Gary's investigative nose began to itch.

"I thought you knew the case."

"I do." Her features brightened and she ran the fingers of one hand across the table. To the left, then to the right. To the left. To the right.

She stilled suddenly, catching herself in the nervous move.

"I want to hear it from you. Step by step. Just in case there's anything I've forgotten."

He frowned, not believing her motivation for a second. "Why?"

"I have a source who's wondering about a child's parentage."

"A kidnapping?" He straightened now, wanting to know every detail.

Sophie shook her head and tucked her wispy brown hair behind her ears. "Not necessarily. Could be mistaken identity."

He leaned forward, close enough that Sophie sat back, pressing herself against the padded bench seat.

"I'm not following you."

She measured his expression, her eyes reading his face. She tipped her head and pressed her lips together, her stare never leaving his. "Off the record?"

Now she had his full attention. "Sure."

"What if a child was presumed dead, but there might be a possibility that child was alive? Where would you start?"

Now Gary was the one who straightened against his seat. "What about the body?"

"No body." Her features tensed.

Gary pursed his lips. "How?"

"Fire."

The images crystallized in his mind. The black-and-white of the burned-out home. The photos of the mother and daughter who had perished in the blaze, the child's remains obliterated by the heat of the inferno.

He'd heard rumor of how crazed Sophie had been after the deaths. Not that he could blame her, but did she really believe anyone could have survived? After five years, hadn't she let go of the grief and moved on?

"You're not talking about a source, are you?"

Her eyes widened, as if the fact he'd seen right through her surprised her. She shook her head.

"What brought this on?"

"I saw someone."

The pain in her voice gripped at his gut and twisted. For a crazy moment, he longed to reach across the table and take her hands. Longed to pull her into his arms and smooth away her heartache. But seven years was a wide void to cover, and he had no intention of bridging that gap.

"Who?"

Sophie shook her head. "No names. Just help me."

Help her? Words Gary thought he'd never hear uttered from Sophie's gorgeous lips. She'd never let herself need anyone, had she?

"Please, Gary." Her eyes pleaded with him now, eradicating any bitter feelings he still held for her. "Tell me where to start."

And so he detailed every step of the Hernandez case. Every inch of the investigation, the identification, the reunion of the kidnapped child with her mother.

As he walked back toward his car, he found it impossible to quiet the whirling thoughts and questions racing through his brain.

Who had Sophie seen? When? Where?

What had sparked her reporter's brain to question the validity of her niece's death?

Then one thought silenced all of the rest.

She'd reached out to him. She'd asked for help.

Maybe Sophie's sharp edges hadn't won out yet after all.

"THOUGHT YOU DIDN'T LIKE these fluff pieces," Cookie said as he drove the WNJZ van across town toward the Alexander home.

"It's not a fluff piece." Sophie wondered

momentarily if her tone sounded as defensive as it felt. "The powers that be loved the profile angle."

She glanced out the window, watching as the South Jersey scenery shifted from row house to duplex to suburban chic. "You have to admit Maggie Alexander is the perfect example of an everyday citizen who's making a difference."

"Her brother's not bad either."

Sophie cringed at her cameraman's teasing tone. When would she learn never to confide in the man? She'd told him about her connection to Gary on the way back to the station after the fund-raiser. Cookie might be quiet behind the camera, but otherwise, look out.

"All I'm saying is that you could do a lot worse."

Sophie traced her finger along the edge of the door handle. "I don't want to *do* anything at all."

"I'm just saying—"

"Can it." She cut him off before he could launch into his standard lecture on love and family and security.

Sophie knew he meant well, but she didn't

need anyone to remind her of how alone she felt in the world, not that she had anyone but herself to blame. She'd had plenty of opportunities for romance. She'd merely chosen not to take them.

She'd watched her mother's dependency on men spiral out of control during her childhood. After her father had deserted their family, her mother had bounced from one man to another—or rather, the men had bounced in and out of their lives.

No one had stayed around long enough for Sophie and Becca to grow attached. Thankfully.

After the two sisters had grown and left home, their mother had done the unthinkable. She'd taken her own life, choosing to leave this world rather than live alone.

Sophie shuttered her heart to the pain that threatened with the memory. She was not her mother, and she'd never allow herself to be that needy. Never.

As far as she was concerned, being alone was safe.

Being in love was not.

She swallowed down the lump that

formed in her throat just at the thought of being in love—at the thought of Gary. She'd seen the look in his eyes during their meeting, felt the question that had hung unspoken over their table.

Why?

Why had she hurt him? Why had she panicked and run when he'd told her he loved her, asked her to marry him?

Why?

She'd asked herself the same question countless times during the past seven years, but the answer had always been the same.

Needing him, loving him, wasn't a risk she was willing to take.

"Here we are." Cookie pulled the news van to a stop in front of the Alexander home.

Sophie took a quick appraisal of the stately structure, noting the coordinated porch furniture and the oversize pots of flowering perennials still in full bloom, hanging on even though the chilly Philadelphia nights had begun to set in during the past few weeks.

As Sophie climbed the steps, the front door snapped open before she could press the doorbell. Ally Alexander smiled up at her, clutching a pink bunny rabbit in one hand and waving with the other.

"Hi. Mommy said you were coming to read a story."

Maggie Alexander's laugh rumbled down the hall from behind her daughter. "Do a story, sweetheart. Not read a story."

She lovingly patted her daughter's head then shook Sophie's hand. "Welcome. We're delighted for this opportunity."

We?

Sophie's unspoken question was answered before she could speak it out loud.

A handsome man stepped to Maggie's side. Sophie squinted, racking her brain for recognition. She knew him from somewhere, but he was most definitely not Maggie's husband, Robert. So who was he?

"Trevor James. Sophie Markham." Maggie gestured between the two of them. "Trevor is my life coach, though he prefers the term *personal adviser.* Did you two get a chance to meet at the party?"

No, they hadn't. But Sophie recognized him now. Life coach to the rich and famous of the Philadelphia region. The man had made quite a name for himself in the elite circle of the business and social sets. In recent months, his face had been on the news almost as much as her own had been.

Sophie extended her hand. "We didn't, but it's a pleasure to meet you now. I've heard quite a lot about you."

"All good, I hope." James gave her hand a quick pump, but held her gaze a fraction of a second too long, sending a frisson of unease skittering across Sophie's nerve endings.

"Naturally." She freed her grip from his.

Tall and lean, he stood at least six foot three. His dark waves fell in a precise cut that Sophie found borderline artificial. He stepped back, allowing Sophie and Maggie to walk ahead of him.

As much as she told herself she was letting her imagination run amok, Sophie swore she could feel his eyes burning into the back of her skull. The tiny hairs at the base of her neck pricked to attention, and she fought the urge to reach back and smooth them.

In a matter of minutes, Cookie completed their setup and locked the necessary lighting into place. Sophie gave silent thanks, not wanting to make small talk with Trevor James any longer than she had to.

She'd lied when she'd thought she hadn't let herself care for anyone since her breakup with Gary. Cookie's friendship and grace under pressure were two things she'd be lost without, and she cared for him. Over the years, the gentle soul had become the father she'd never known.

He shot her a wink. "Ready when you are, Ms. Markham."

She rolled her eyes at his use of formality, knowing he was the only one in the room who could see her, then she turned her attention to Maggie.

Trevor James sat at the woman's side, his obviously practiced smile glued in place on his chiseled face.

Even though Sophie had done her best to gently suggest the piece would be more genuine if her life coach was not in the shot, Maggie had insisted.

An emotion shone in James's icy eyes, an emotion Sophie couldn't quite put her finger on. Smugness? Confidence? A certainty that he'd get his way no matter what?

She shook off her instinctive dislike of the man and began the interview. She'd no sooner begun than Ally popped into the living room, launching herself into her mother's lap.

"Sorry." Maggie gripped her daughter's hand and marched her toward the kitchen. She returned a few moments later. "She's just excited. If she stays with her coloring books, we'll be safe."

But no more than a few minutes passed before Ally repeated her performance.

Each time the girl appeared, Sophie found herself more and more distracted by the assuredness that had begun to settle into her bones.

Ally Alexander was her niece. Professional objectivity be damned. Robin had somehow survived the fire and had been adopted by the Alexanders.

As crazy as the theory sounded, Sophie's gut knew she was right.

Her head knew.

Her heart knew.

And she'd do whatever it took to get her niece back.

She stifled the gasp that threatened to burst

from her lips. Fought the urge to bundle the girl into her arms and bury her face in the baby-soft hair. She battled down her desire to press her lips to the butterfly birthmark, just as she'd done the day Robin had been born.

"Sophie." Cookie's voice broke through her thoughts. "Earth to Sophie."

"Sorry," she mumbled, reaching for the notepad on her lap onto which she'd scribbled her interview questions.

"No, I'm sorry," Maggie replied. "I'm afraid my daughter's a bit wound up today. She doesn't want to miss anything."

Sophie tipped her head, listening to the sweet notes of Ally's singing coming from the kitchen. "Would she like to watch us?"

Maggie's expression brightened. "She'd love it, but I don't know how we'd ever get her to sit still or be quiet."

Sophie reached down into her bag and pulled out a rainbow-colored lollipop. She kept a bag of the sweet treats handy for occasions just like this one.

"I used to be a Girl Scout," she teased. "Is she allowed to have this?"

"Always prepared." Maggie nodded and

took the offered treat, then called out to Ally. The young girl's navy-blue eyes grew to the size of saucers as she spied the candy. "You have to sit still and be quiet. Can you do that?" Maggie asked.

Ally grew very serious, nodding her head as if the sight of the lollipop had put her into a trance.

A few moments later, she settled happily across the room, licking her treat and quietly watching her mother's interview.

Sophie shut out the questions screaming through her mind and immersed herself in the task at hand. She methodically fired questions at Maggie and redirected the interview as necessary to gather enough statements and reactions to edit the final piece.

She was deep in the zone when Ally let out a squeal and dashed across the room to where a newcomer stood, wordlessly watching the scene before him.

Cookie cut the camera light and Sophie turned, her heart lodging in her throat at the sight of Ally bundled into Gary Barksdale's arms. He'd shaved today and the dimples winking out from his cheeks reawakened long-dead memories of lazy afternoon walks and long talks that had lasted into the wee hours of the morning.

The mental pictures grabbed Sophie's heart and squeezed.

She swallowed down the unwanted tangle of emotions and plastered on her most professional smile.

"Sorry to interrupt," Gary said with a wink. "Thought you'd be done by now."

WHEN MAGGIE HAD PHONED to let Gary know Sophie was on her way over to do a feature spot, he couldn't resist watching. He knew his sister's game, but so what? She had designs on putting him in close proximity with Sophie, no doubt wanting to rekindle the spark of what they'd once shared.

The diversion had fit perfectly into his day. His next piece wasn't due until tomorrow, and after he'd spent the morning reviewing the photos and stories that had covered Rebecca and Robin Markham's deaths, he had to admit Sophie might be on to something with her theory.

Seeing her again would give him a chance

to dig more deeply into just what had awakened her suspicions.

At the time of the fire, the investigators' determination that the absence of the child's remains needn't be questioned had been acceptable. But the case had been unprecedented. Shouldn't that alone have raised a note of doubt?

The cause of the fire had been ruled accidental. Gary realized that point was crucial. Any sign of foul play would have raised a red flag, but there had been none.

End of story. Closed case.

Closed, at least, until Sophie's questions had kicked his investigative brain into overdrive. The what-ifs had been rattling around inside his skull all day.

As he watched Sophie now, he took stock of how far she'd come with her career. He remembered the day she'd done her first live report for WNJZ. He'd watched every second, had followed her career from graduation forward. As much as he tried to deny it, Gary had always been sure of one thing.

For him, Sophie Markham would always be the one that got away. Hands down. No matter that she had broken his heart, he'd never been able to shake the depth of what they'd shared for however briefly they'd shared it.

Ally had begun to alternate between licking her lollipop and singing. Maggie shot Gary the evil eye and he smiled. He recognized that nonverbal cue. He held out his hand to his niece and tipped his chin toward the kitchen.

She smiled, tucked her tiny fingers into his hand and skipped all the way down the hall. Ah, the wonders of refined sugar.

Ally settled at the kitchen table and lost herself in her coloring books. Gary absent-mindedly nodded encouragement as she showed him page after page of brightly colored scribbles. All the while, however, his brain clicked through everything Sophie had said at their meeting.

She'd seen someone.

So at some point in the recent past, Sophie had seen someone who looked enough like what she thought her niece would look like to raise her suspicions.

A child.

Ally bounced away from the table, having

lost interest in her works of art. He watched as she danced around the kitchen, swinging her lollipop as if it were a magic wand, her short brown hair bouncing with the motion. Her blue eyes sparkling with happiness.

A child the right age and coloring.

Gary's throat tightened as he flashed on the images of Robin Markham's photos. The little girl who would have been five years old.

Just like Ally.

Gary had given Sophie step-by-step instructions on what to look for. Fingerprints. Bone structure. Eye color.

"Wanna lick, Uncle Gary?" Ally waved the lollipop in his face.

He shook his head. "No thanks, kiddo."

"Miss Sophie gave it to me." She gestured dramatically as if he didn't know what he was missing. "It's good."

DNA.

The puzzle pieces flew into place.

Disbelief and fury tangled inside him as he turned away from Ally and headed back to where Sophie and Maggie were finishing up.

Sophie had met Ally at the fund-raiser, then she'd sought out Gary only because of his relation to his niece. Not because she'd needed him. She'd needed his connection. Furthermore she'd used him for information on how to ID a kidnapped child.

What a fool he'd been.

How typical of Sophie Markham to walk back into his life without so much as an apology or an explanation of the past. He should have known she had her own agenda.

Well, he had a news flash for the woman.

If Sophie thought she could use him against his own family, she had another think coming. And when she lifted her gaze to his, the look of surprise on her pretty features told him she knew exactly what he was thinking.

Chapter Three

Sophie straightened, willing herself not to wilt beneath the fury emanating from Gary's gaze. He crooked his finger, and she turned to Maggie, pasting on a phony smile.

"You were wonderful. I'll be sure to let you know when your segment's going to air." She tipped her head toward Gary. "I think your brother needs me for a moment."

Maggie eyed her warily as she excused herself, and Sophie wondered just how much the woman knew about her and Gary's shared past.

The question evaporated when she stepped into the kitchen and took in the sight of Gary, hands on hips, color blazing in his cheeks.

He gave Ally's shoulder a pat and nodded

toward the hall. "I think your mommy's calling you."

The little girl took off like a shot, leaving her lollipop glued to a page in her coloring book.

"Just who in the hell do you think you are?"

Gary's words hit her like a slap, and she adopted a tone of indignation. "I don't know what you're talking about."

But she did. She knew in that instant exactly what he was talking about. The man wasn't an award-winning journalist without reason. He'd put the pieces together and knew she'd been talking about Ally when she'd questioned him the day before.

"Do you want to start, or should I?"

Sophie flinched. "Why don't you." She wasn't a fool. She could formulate her response as he spoke. No sense giving away any information he hadn't already figured out.

"You spot my niece at the fund-raiser, learn she's adopted, and decide—for whatever reason—she's your niece." He dropped his voice low and stood so close Sophie could feel the heat of his anger.

"Then you butter me up for a how-to on identifying a kidnapped child." His voice cracked with emotion and he looked away momentarily.

"What do you think?" he continued. "Do you think my sister and brother-in-law stole your sister's child?"

He gripped Sophie's shoulders and gave her a quick shake. A whisper of anxiousness filtered through her. She knew he'd never hurt her. He wasn't that type of man, but she'd never seen the depth of fury in his eyes she saw there now.

"Your niece is dead, Sophie," he continued. "I'm sorry, but she's gone. Forever. Stay away from my family."

No, Sophie screamed silently. Robin wasn't dead. She was in the next room singing to the woman who had adopted her.

Someone cleared his throat, and Sophie and Gary both turned quickly to spot Trevor James standing in the doorway. Instead of showing any concern over his intrusion, he instead wore an expression of annoyance, as if they were in his way.

He tipped his chin toward the refrigerator. "Need to grab one of my beverages."

They both watched wordlessly as he crossed

the room, opened the appliance door and took out a bottle of vitamin-enhanced water.

"Carry on," he said glibly as he headed back out into the hall.

Gary's eyes narrowed, focused on James's back. "Pompous—"

"Look at her birthmark," Sophie interrupted, forcing her voice through her throat, now tight with emotion. She kept her speaking volume low, not wanting to be overheard by the others down the hall. "Robin had an identical mark. *Identical.*"

The heat of her determination fired in her cheeks and she knew she'd lost all semblance of professional cool. She could care less.

"People can have similar birthmarks." Gary dropped his hands to his sides and stepped away from her.

Sophie's frustration soared, overwhelming her. She jammed her finger into his chest, flinching when he caught her hand in his fist.

"Not similar. Identical." She pressed the point, refusing to be intimidated by anything Gary said or did.

"It's impossible." He leaned close, not letting go of her hand. "That little girl out there is the light of my sister's life. She's my niece. *My* niece." He shook his head. "Not yours."

Sophie wriggled her fingers free. "What if you're wrong? Are you willing to live with not knowing? I know you, Gary. You live for the story. Live for the truth.

"Are you going to look me in the eye and tell me you can walk away from the possibility I may be right?"

Gary stood his ground, not giving her the satisfaction of so much as a blink.

Yet another male throat cleared and Sophie snapped her attention to the doorway. Cookie leaned against the doorjamb, the look on his face making it abundantly clear he'd heard every word.

Sophie grimaced. She could only hope their voices hadn't carried to where Maggie and her daughter sat.

"I hate to interrupt," Cook said. "We've got to go. Breaking story."

Sophie welcomed the excuse to walk away from the argument, even though her anger had reached its boiling point. Blood roared in her ears, and she was certain her normally pale complexion was flush with color.

Gary reached for her arm as she passed, but she dodged his touch. "We're not through discussing this," he called after her, anger heavy in his voice.

Sophie paused at the doorway, turning back to pin him with her gaze. "That's where you're wrong. This discussion is most definitely over."

But as she headed out of the house toward the van, she knew Gary would never let the topic drop that easily. He'd make contact again, and before he did she had better get her thoughts—and emotions—in check.

HOURS LATER, JOHN COOK PULLED the news van back into the WNJZ parking lot. Sophie didn't know about the older man, but she was exhausted and hungry. Her head had been pounding ever since she'd left the Alexanders' home, and spending seven hours covering a hostage situation hadn't done much to ease her tension.

"Want to tell me about it?" Cookie asked.

"What? My headache?" Sophie rolled her neck, then massaged her pounding temples. She could feel Cook's visual scrutiny, but she squeezed her eyes shut, hoping he'd take a hint.

"Whatever you and Gary Barksdale were arguing about earlier."

Apparently Cookie wasn't going to let this one go without forcing the issue.

"Sounded pretty intense. Did I hear you mention Becca and Robin?"

Sophie spun on him, gracing him with one of her trademark glares. "How about if I give you a transcript? Would that ease your curiosity?"

Her venom didn't make the man flinch, not in the least. He knew her too well, knew all of her acts of bravado were nothing more than smoke and mirrors.

"Feel better?" He crooked a gray brow.

"No." She slouched in her seat, regretting her inappropriate outburst. "Sorry. You didn't deserve that."

"Nope." He shook his head and patted her arm. "I didn't, but I'm glad I could be here to take the heat. Now, are you going to tell me what's going on, or am I going to have to use the wide-angle lens the next time I film you?"

It was his favorite threat, and it never failed to make Sophie smile.

"Anything but that." She pulled herself

upright in the seat and took a deep breath. "You have to give me your word you won't tell a soul."

Cookie nodded. "You know you don't have to remind me of that."

"You're right." Sophie swallowed before she continued. "Did you notice the Alexanders' daughter?"

Cookie let loose with a chuckle that rumbled the windows of the van. "The whirlwind with the lollipop, the coloring books and the off-note singing?"

Sophie nodded. "I think she could be Robin."

Cook blinked, then his eyes narrowed. Silence stretched between them. "How?"

Sophie breathed a sigh of relief. He knew her well enough to know she'd have thought through every possible angle before making such a statement.

"You remember there were no remains, right?"

He nodded without saying a word, lines of concern etching the corners of his eyes.

"Did I ever tell you about her birthmark?"

Cookie shook his head.

"A butterfly," Sophie continued. "A perfect

butterfly." She pointed to the nape of her neck. "Right here."

"Just like the Alexander girl," Cook said softly.

Sophie met his curious gaze and nodded. "And she's five years old."

"The same age Robin would be."

"And she's adopted."

He gripped the steering wheel as if the news had thrown him off balance. "So you'll pull the adoption records and take it from there?"

"Yeah." Sophie blew out a tired sigh. "I will. I'm compelled to check this out. I have no choice."

"What if it turns out she's not your niece?"

"Then at least I'll know for sure." She breathed in deeply, realizing she wasn't prepared for that possibility. She'd already decided she was right in her assumption.

"And if she is your niece?" His tone dropped low and intent. "Are you going to take her away from the only home she's ever known?"

Sophie opened her mouth to answer, but then fell silent. She hadn't really thought about the situation from that perspective. Bringing Robin home was going to be a long and difficult road. She could handle it, though. She had to. For Becca.

"I'll do whatever it takes to make things right."

"What if what's right is leaving that girl where she is?"

Disbelief knotted in Sophie's throat. John Cook was the last person she expected opposition from. "Whose side are you on, Cook?"

He patted her knee. "Yours, honey. You know that. I just want to make sure you've really thought this thing through before you do anything rash." The gray brows met in a peak. "You'll be careful?"

"Always."

He gave her a quick wink. "Okay. Then let's get you out of this van and on your way home. It's been a long day."

"I have to run in for a few things." Sophie shrugged into her jacket as she stepped down from the van. "Want me to grab anything for you?"

"I'm good." He shook his head and grinned. "I'm just going to straighten up here then head home. I'll see you bright and early."

"You got it." Sophie paused for a split

second, then stepped close and planted a kiss on his cheek.

His blush was evident even in the shadows of the dark parking lot. "What was that for?"

Sophie shrugged. "Just because."

"You're not getting soft on me are you?" His tone had taken on a teasing note. "I know how particular you are about keeping your cool."

"Never." She released a quick laugh as she hurried across the parking lot.

Getting soft? Not hardly.

She'd worked too hard for too long to earn her reputation as one cool reporter under fire.

But cool or not, right now she was emotionally wrung out, wanting only to gather a few personal items and put this day behind her.

HER PRODUCER HAD SIDETRACKED Sophie when she'd dashed inside to grab her date book. Now, fifteen minutes later, she was beyond exhaustion, ready for a hot bath, a glass of wine and sleep. Lots of sleep.

All worries about Gary Barksdale and Ally

Alexander could wait until morning. She wasn't capable of additional coherent thought tonight.

Forty-eight hours ago, her life had been status quo. Now her reality had been tilted on its axis.

If Ally was her niece, not only had Robin survived, but she'd been put up for adoption. By whom? And why? And if whoever had taken her had planned their actions, had the fire really been an accident?

She shook her head. She was overtired and letting her imagination get carried away.

She weaved between the parked cars in the lot and stopped dead in her tracks at the site of the van. The side door sat wide open, just as it had been when she'd said goodnight to Cookie.

A shiver whispered down her spine, and she quickened her pace. What was taking him so long? Was something wrong with the truck? With Cookie?

She had her answer the second she got close enough to see into the van. Cookie lay sprawled across the equipment on the floor of the truck, one arm bent beneath him at an unnatural angle, blood flowing from the corner of his mouth.

"Cook." The word slid across her lips, barely audible.

Her heart lurched in her chest.

She scrambled into the van, checking for a pulse and breathing a sigh of relief when she found one—weak, but beating.

"Don't you worry. I'm going to get you help."

She watched the slow rise and fall of his chest, satisfying herself he was able to breathe on his own. She shrugged out of her jacket, bundled it on top of him, then dumped the contents of her purse to locate her cell phone, not wanting to leave his side long enough to reach the van's two-way radio.

She hit the speed-dial button for 911. "WNJZ parking lot. We need help ASAP."

But before the voice on the other end of the line could respond, something knocked the phone from Sophie's hand. She twisted, raising her hands defensively, but she was too late.

Her assailant backhanded her across the side of her face, then hoisted her, kicking and screaming from the van.

The masked man pinned her to the asphalt, his knee in her chest. Her face throbbed from where he'd struck her, and her legs protested at the way they'd been twisted beneath her.

When he slapped a piece of heavy tape over her mouth, bile rose in her throat. Her only hope now was that help for Cookie would arrive in time to save her.

She fought to scramble to her feet, but felt the back of her attacker's hand against her cheek again. This time when she fell, her attacker dragged her around the far side of the van, headed toward the deserted lot of the soon-to-be-demolished hotel next door.

She had to break free. Had to. All of her self-defense training screamed through her brain.

Don't let him take you to a second location. Fight him. Fight him.

She kicked, working to free her feet from her pumps. Once the shoes fell away, she fought to hook a foot on a rock, in a hole, anything that might slow their forward progress.

Panic squeezed at her insides and she struggled to remain coherent.

Focus, Sophie. Focus.

If she lost control of her senses now, she might very well end up raped…or far worse.

Sirens sounded and Sophie dared hope she might survive—unless her attacker had dragged her so far out of sight the authorities would never find her.

Icy cold terror tangled with her panic.

What if no one looked for her?

She'd dumped her purse before she made the call. Anyone responding to the scene would know she'd been there. And her coworkers knew she'd never leave Cook alone and injured.

Cookie.

Her attacker tightened his grip, dragging her forcibly farther and farther away from the lot. She continued to wiggle and kick, doing her best to break free, to slow him down, to frustrate him.

Sophie's heart twisted in her chest at the thought of Cookie injured and bleeding.

Determination welled inside her. She had to find a way out of this, had to find a way to escape.

Her assailant dropped her to the hard ground, and the back of her head connected with packed dirt.

The sirens grew nearer and he straightened, looking in both directions. When he bent down, putting his face near hers, she swung at him wildly, but he pinned her arms down effortlessly. She brought her knee up, hoping she'd hit his groin, but missing her mark.

Panic surged through her every muscle and nerve ending. How would she survive this? How would she escape? He was too big, too strong.

Just as she'd begun to accept her fate, he spoke.

"Consider this a warning."

The cold edge of the man's voice cut through the night air, freezing Sophie in mid-struggle.

"Next time, you won't live to talk about it."

He released his grip on her arms and Sophie struggled to sit up, to wriggle away.

This time, when his hand connected with her face and her head slammed against the hard dirt, Sophie's vision faded.

Then turned to black.

Chapter Four

The whine grew louder and louder, nearer and nearer. Sophie struggled to open her eyes. She couldn't shake the pitch-black and fought against it. Her eyelids felt as though someone had pasted them shut and her cheekbone felt as though it had been shattered into a million pieces.

"She's coming around," a female voice said, close.

A hand pressed against her arm and she tried to jerk away, but her body didn't want to respond to her brain's signal. She recognized the whine now, loud and piercing. A siren.

The metallic mix of fear and blood lingering in her mouth brought the memory of what had happened crashing back. She'd been attacked, and Cookie had been badly beaten.

She struggled against the hand holding her, wanting to get away, needing to get away.

"Settle down. You're going to be fine." The female voice spoke again. "Almost there."

Sophie forced her eyes open. The woman was nothing more than a shadowy blur until Sophie managed a blink that brought her surroundings into focus.

The inside of an ambulance.

"How's Cook?" She managed to push the words through her shock and pain.

The paramedic hesitated before she answered, and Sophie's mind immediately jumped to the worst-case scenario. "Is he—"

"He's pretty banged up." The paramedic gave a slight nod. "I'll try to get an update for you once we get you settled inside."

The vehicle jerked to a stop and the back doors flew open. The next several moments were a blur of voices, antiseptic smells and ceiling tiles whizzing past over Sophie's head as they rushed her into the emergency room triage area.

She'd covered plenty of stories from outside these same doors, but this was the first time she'd had occasion to be the center of a medical team's attention. She prayed it would be the last.

Her head felt as though it were about to explode and she closed her eyes, willing the pain to go away, but fighting to stay conscious. She wanted to be sharp enough to find out if Cookie was all right, to find out what had happened.

The masked face flashed through her memory and she shuddered. Why had they been attacked? And by whom?

Her mind wanted to leap from the table and chase the story, look at the evidence and piece together the facts, but she knew better. She was starting to feel everything now. Her battered face. Battered legs. Battered head.

Her mind might be up for the chase, but her body was a long way from cooperating.

GARY DIDN'T LOOK UP from the clippings on the Markham deaths when the shadow fell across his desk. He didn't know who or what wanted something, but right now he didn't give a damn about anything but proving Sophie Markham wrong.

There was no way in hell Ally was her deceased niece, Robin. *No way.*

"What?" he snarled.

"Another television-station attack."

Gary snapped his attention away from the papers and looked up at the serious expression plastered on Randy Simpson's face—not that the man's expression was ever anything but serious.

"Which one?"

"WNJZ."

Randy had been covering the local crime beat for as long as Gary could remember and had helped him trace down the facts on the Markham fire. The man had become immune to reactions. He delivered the news of the attack as if such an incident were an everyday occurrence.

"Injuries?" Gary asked, doing his best to ignore the twinge of dread deep in his gut.

"Two." Simpson nodded. "Cameraman named John Cook and Sophie Markham. Thought you'd be interested since you're digging into her sister's death."

Gary scraped back his chair, fishing in his desk drawer for his keys. "How bad?"

"They're on their way to PCOM. I'm headed over."

"I'll follow you."

They set off across the newsroom at a quick clip.

"Think it's the same guy who hit WPVI and KYW last year?" Gary's standard breaking-case adrenaline translated itself into a quickened pulse. Yet this time, his heartbeat was due to more than just a fresh story.

This time, the woman attacked had been none other than Sophie Markham. She'd been nothing but a memory until yesterday and now she'd appeared front and center on his radar screen.

He might be mad as hell at her right now, but he'd never wish her harm.

Two of the top female reporters at competing stations had been attacked several months prior, and the cops had never made an arrest, chalking it up to crazed fans. The reporters had each suffered superficial cuts and bruising, and the city's major stations had all upped their security.

As he dropped into the driver's seat of his

Mustang and twisted on the ignition, he could only hope Sophie's injuries had been superficial as well.

"YOUR FIANCÉ IS HERE to see you."

Sophie frowned, wincing instantly at the pain the facial movement caused. "Fiancé?"

The older woman smiled brightly. "I'll go get him."

Fiancé? Who on earth would use that line to get in to see her?

Her pulse pounded in her ears and she reached for the call button. She'd managed to grip the cord and was about to signal for the nurse to come back when Gary Barksdale appeared in the door.

"Fiancé?" she said, her voice weak, but tinged with disbelief.

He shrugged, his forced smile not hiding the worry painted across his handsome features. "Hey, I'm nothing if not resourceful." He stopped next to the bed, reaching toward Sophie's face, but dropping his hand to the side rail instead.

Disappointment whispered through her inexplicably.

"You hanging in there?"

He forced a bright note into his voice, but he couldn't fool Sophie. She knew she must look like hell, and the concern blazing in Gary's eyes confirmed her suspicions about just how bad she looked.

She nodded, grimacing again at the slightest movement. "Other than the fact my brain feels a bit loose, I'm okay. And they tell me I still have all my teeth. That's got to count for something."

"I heard Cook's going to be all right, too."

Tears swam in her vision and she blinked them away. Vulnerability was one attribute she had no intention of showing Gary. "He looked so bad when I found him." She swallowed, working to steady her voice. "I think he'll be out of work for a while."

Gary's brows lifted. "I don't think you and those bruises will be on camera anytime soon, either."

Her stomach did a quick flip-flop. Just how bad *did* she look? But Gary was right. She just hadn't thought that far ahead yet.

Being off-camera would give her more time to investigate both her attack and the Alexander adoption, not that she was about to share that thought with Gary at the moment. She didn't have the energy to launch into another argument right now.

"Any idea of who might have done this?" Gary dragged a plastic chair close to the side of the bed.

She warmed at the instant sense of security his presence provided, then mentally chastised herself. She'd never been one to depend on anyone—least of all Gary. Not even for something as simple as company in a lonely hospital room.

From what she understood, Cookie had a waiting room full of people praying for him. Wife, children, grandchildren. Envious tears stung her eyes and she willed them away.

Some people were meant to be part of a large family. Cookie was, and he deserved every bit of it. She wasn't. Rebecca and Robin had been the only family she'd had, yet one day they'd been part of her life, and the next they'd been gone. Seemingly lost forever.

"Sophie?" Gary's eyebrows snapped together. "Any idea?"

She swallowed down the lump in her throat

and faced him, faced the memory of the attack. The feel of her attacker's hands on her face, around her neck.

"I keep trying to run the possibilities through my head," she answered. "But I'm not coming up with anything."

Gary's eyes narrowed. "Working on any big stories right now?"

She tried to shake her head, but caught herself before she made the move. "I just wrapped up a big piece on city council. Nothing else going on."

"Anger anyone?"

She smiled. "I always anger someone."

No KIDDING. AND HE'D LIKE to know just who she'd angered to end up on the receiving end of the beating she'd taken.

He couldn't help but wince as he took inventory of the purple-and-blue marks covering the side of Sophie's face. A small bandage covered what he imagined were stitches just next to one eyebrow.

Had she pushed someone too far, or was this attack related to the previous two? If so, the guy was escalating. Sophie's injuries

were definitely more severe than minor cuts
and bruises, and this time John Cook had
been attacked as well. The two prior attacks
had occurred as the reporters had walked
alone to their cars at night.

He could pull the files on the first two
attacks and look for similarities. Then he
could pull her most recent reports. Maybe
she was overlooking a story that might have
pissed someone off, though the city-council
piece was a definite possibility.

He caught himself partway through his
standard investigative thought process,
giving himself a mental slap. He had his own
pieces to work on. This one belonged to
Simpson. Gary needed to step away from
both Sophie Markham and her story.

"You didn't have to come here." Her soft
voice filtered into his thoughts.

He nodded. "I know that. But I wanted to
make sure you were all right."

A twinge of color fired in her cheeks and
he wondered, not for the first time, if she'd
ever regretted the way she'd walked away.

He shoved the question out of his mind

before it could take root. Sophie's thoughts were none of his concern. He'd written the woman off years before, and he'd be better off if he kept her there.

His interest in her now was personal, but it had nothing to do with their one-time romance. His loyalty to his family demanded he keep abreast of any digging she did into his niece's adoption.

He couldn't resist just one more question about the attack. "Anything distinguishing about the attacker?"

Sophie shook her head then paled. "He told me to consider this a warning."

"Your attacker?"

She nodded.

"Any idea about what?"

"No. I keep running possible reasons through my head, but I can't seem to make sense of any of it."

Gary drew in a deep breath, processing the threat. "The police have any ideas?"

"They think it could be the same guy who hit WPVI and KYW last year." She shook her head. "They're going through all of my recent stories, just the same."

"Have you been assigned anything controversial?"

She closed her eyes, and Gary wondered if it might be too soon to be interrogating her. She'd had one hell of a night, and probably wanted nothing more than to rest.

She sighed, the sound full of disappointment. "I had a huge exposé on the parking authority planned, but now that will have to wait. Just watch. One of the other stations will beat me to it and I'll be out of an exclusive."

Gary nodded, all the while thinking Sophie Markham's life really did revolve around her job. She'd mentioned nothing other than her on-air time and stories that would be impacted by her injuries.

"Anything else?" he asked.

She blew out a sigh and studied his face, her eyes suddenly shuttered once more. "The only other thing I'm working on now is personal."

Anger pushed against the sympathy he'd felt a moment earlier. "My family?"

She nodded.

Gary shook his head. "But you and I are the only two people who know about that."

"And Cook."

"He obviously didn't injure himself, and as much as I wouldn't mind knocking some sense into you, I was at the newsroom all night."

The corners of her eyes softened. "I have to know the truth, Gary. What if I'm right?"

His anger intensified, edging out any compassion he'd felt for her due to the attack. "You're not."

She visibly flinched at his harsh tone.

Gary pushed away from her bed and stepped a few paces away, working to control the fury building inside him. "You should be more worried about who did this—" he gestured toward her battered face "—than about trying to destroy my family."

"I'm not out to destroy them."

He closed the gap between them, leaning over the side of the bed. "Aren't you?"

Sophie's dark eyes widened, then pressed shut. "I'm too tired to argue with you now."

"Convenient." Gary straightened and turned toward the door. "I'm glad you're all right. Give Cook my best wishes."

"He said that next time I wouldn't live to talk about it."

Her words caught him just as he reached the doorway. He hesitated momentarily, turning to look back at her. She appeared tiny in the bed, the pristine hospital sheet tucked around her slender body, a blood-pressure cuff wrapped around her upper arm.

"You told the cops?"

She nodded. Something in her expression stopped Gary cold.

"What?"

"What if your sister overheard us arguing?" She pressed her lips together before she continued. "We weren't exactly whispering at each other in the kitchen."

His concern over Sophie's attack gave way to a fresh wave of anger. "Are you trying to blame this attack on my sister? Do you honestly think she'd be behind something like this?"

She didn't answer, and her silence infuriated him like no words could have.

He didn't dignify her suggestion with further conversation, instead heading out into the hall and straight for the exit.

While he couldn't wait to put as much distance between him and Sophie Markham as possible, he'd have to see her again. Have to keep an eye on her.

The woman was more delusional than he'd thought previously, and there was only one thing to do. Uncover the truth and wrap up the loose ends before Sophie and her wild theories could do any damage to his sister's family.

If that meant staying close to Ms. Markham, so be it.

IT HAD BEEN AFTER MIDNIGHT when Gary had left the hospital. As much as he'd wanted to go straight to his sister and brother-in-law's house, he knew they'd be asleep. Instead, he waited until the morning, deciding he could catch them at the breakfast table before they each started their day.

As the morning sun rose higher in the sky, he sat in front of their house considering his options. He could go inside and tell them about Sophie's suspicions, or he could drive away, letting them remain blissfully ignorant of the woman's ridiculous accusations. After all, sooner or later she'd realize she was grasping at straws.

There was no way Ally could be Robin

Markham. The Markham infant had perished. Remains or no remains. He'd pulled the old notes again after he'd left the hospital and the findings from the fire investigator had left no room for doubt.

Apparently, the blaze had burned long enough and hot enough to obliterate the remains of an infant.

Nonetheless, a cold realization settled over him. Maggie and Robert deserved to know the woman was out to prove their daughter was her own flesh and blood.

Gary took a deep breath and climbed out of his car. As usual, his sister's home was immaculate—from the mailbox at the curb to the flowers that lined the porch. He bypassed the front steps, instead heading around the side of the house to the kitchen door. He knocked once, then pushed the unlocked door open.

Robert looked up over his morning paper and nodded. "Gary."

"Breakfast?" Maggie asked. "I just made some eggs. There's plenty." She tipped her head toward a vacant seat. "I'll fix you a plate."

As usual, his sister was in overdrive. The

woman hadn't sat still since the moment she was born. Now that she'd been working with life coach Trevor James, she'd become even more driven.

Personally, Gary thought James's whole act was a load of crap, but he wasn't about to share that thought with Maggie. She and plenty of other area movers and shakers thought James's word was gospel.

Gary sighed inwardly. He shouldn't complain. In the months after his nephew's sudden death, his sister had shut down physically and mentally. If seeing her happy and productive meant putting up with the arrogant Trevor James, so be it.

"Where's the munchkin?" he asked as Maggie handed him a mug of black coffee.

"She decided her stuffed animals needed rearranging." Robert smiled. "I think she's got her mother's gift for redecorating."

"Women," Gary mumbled just before he took a long drink of the hot coffee. "I need to talk to you two about something while she's out of earshot."

He hated to start off their day with this news, but if big ears was out of range, this was his chance to speak to them without Ally overhearing.

Maggie slipped into a seat. "Sounds serious. You all right?"

"This have anything to do with that reporter you used to date?" One of Robert's dark brows lifted. "Just saw a bit on the metro page about her attack."

So his sister hadn't wasted any time filling Robert in on Gary's past.

His sister shot her husband a glare, as if he'd been told not to repeat what she'd told him. She shook her head. "Can't imagine who on earth would do such a thing."

"You'd be surprised." Gary shrugged. "Sometimes being in the public eye makes you a target."

He hesitated, trying to think of a gentle way to say what he had to say. "I didn't come here to talk to you about that." He leaned forward, first looking into Robert's eyes, then settling on his sister's. "I came into some information that you need to know about."

Maggie's expectant features slipped into a frown. "Such as?"

Delivering this piece of news was like ripping off a Band-Aid, Gary decided. All he had to do was talk fast and get the sting over with as quickly as possible.

"Sophie Markham is convinced Ally is her biological niece."

Maggie's mouth gaped open and her cheeks paled.

"Did you hear us arguing yesterday?" Gary continued, pushing past the shock plastered all over his sister's and brother-in-law's faces.

He had to ask. Had to know whether or not Sophie had any grounds for thinking his family had something to do with her attack.

His sister shook her head slowly from side to side. "I wanted to give you your privacy."

"Wasn't her niece killed?" Robert's legal training had apparently taken over, shifting his thought process automatically to a line of questioning.

Gary nodded. "That's what the authorities said, but no body was ever found."

"Exactly what is she alleging?" Robert's expression had grown intent, dark.

Gary sat back against the chair's hard back. "She's alleging that somehow her niece was removed from the house either during or before the fire and put up for adoption."

Robert squinted. Maggie's features crumpled.

She turned to study her husband. "Surely there's no possible way...Robert?"

He shook his head. "None. Ally came to us through her birth mother. There's no way she could be the same child."

Gary dragged a hand across his face. "The thing is this. Her coloring is the same. Her age is correct. And she's got an identical birthmark to the Markham girl."

"Children have similar birthmarks all the time, don't they?" Maggie's voice had climbed a few octaves, and Gary could read the panic in her eyes.

He hated putting her through this hell. Hated planting the seed of doubt that somehow Ally might be Robin Markham— that somehow her adoption might have been illegal.

He softened his tone. "I'd think the odds might be fairly long for a mark that specific, but you never know. Anything's possible."

Robert straightened, pulling himself taller in his seat. "What do we do to stop her?"

"What about agreeing to a DNA test?" Gary measured their stunned reactions as he asked the question.

Maggie pushed back her chair and shot across the room to the counter as if someone had pushed the Eject button. "This is preposterous. I won't have our daughter subjected to testing just because of some woman's crazy theories. I don't care that she's a local celebrity. I just—"

Her last thought was interrupted by the sound of high-pitched singing out in the hall. With that, Ally appeared, dragging a large stuffed elephant behind her.

"Uncle Gary!" She climbed into his lap and wrapped her arms around his neck, her back to Maggie.

"I won't have it," Maggie mouthed, tears glistening in her eyes.

Robert left his seat and moved to his wife's side, wrapping one arm protectively around her shoulders. "The test would be the quickest way to put this behind us." His features softened as he faced Maggie. "The sooner we comply, the sooner the entire matter is over and done with."

"What if it leaks to the press?" Maggie's gaze widened. "True or not, they'd have a field day."

"Field day." Ally's soft words brushed against Gary's cheek as she pushed out of his grasp and wiggled to the floor. The elephant landed on the ceramic tile and she walked to where her parents stood, then planted her little fists on her hips. "Juice, please."

A tear slid down Maggie's cheek.

"We'll make that a condition." Robert's voice went firmer now, more sure of himself. "If she wants our cooperation, she'll have to agree." He planted a quick kiss on Maggie's cheek, then hoisted Ally into the air. "Juice it is."

Gary couldn't help but note his brother-in-law's tight voice, choked with emotion, nor could he tear his eyes from the back of his niece's neck.

A perfect butterfly.

He wasn't sure what the odds were for identical birthmarks, but he intended to find out. He'd stop by the newsroom, put in a few hours and see what research he could tap into.

Then, he'd bring Sophie up to date on the Alexanders' conditions.

And no matter what transpired, he knew one thing for certain. He'd do whatever he had to do to protect Ally—and the parents who'd loved her for the past five years.

Chapter Five

Sophie had been discharged the next morning, but had checked in on Cook before she'd headed home for a two-week leave of absence. He'd not yet regained consciousness, but his vitals were strong and the doctors were encouraged.

His wife, Anne, hadn't left his side since he'd been admitted the night before. She'd been cradling Cook's hand in her own, speaking to him in an even, soothing tone of voice when Sophie had left them.

He'd be fine. He was strong-willed and healthy and he'd make a full recovery. He had to.

As Sophie sat now in the middle of her guest room bed, she couldn't help but feel responsible for what had happened, as if she'd touched on a story that had put both their lives at risk. But what?

Gary was right—the attack couldn't have anything to do with her suspicions about the Alexander child. She'd been thinking crazy, and she owed him an apology for accusing Maggie of having anything to do with what had happened.

The investigating officers had paid her another visit before her discharge, once again walking her through the night before, step by step. Everything had happened so quickly, her memories were no more than a series of rapid-fire, blurred images.

Yet, she'd never forget the man's voice, even though he'd disguised it somehow, she was sure.

He'd been tall—probably Gary's height or a bit taller, yet not as solidly built. No. Her attacker had been lean—lean, but strong. Like someone who might practice martial arts or yoga. Not a bodybuilder.

She hadn't been able to provide much more in the way of description, and she could read the disappointment in the detectives' faces. She'd given them very little to go on.

The man had worn not only a mask, but also gloves, and he'd left them nothing in the way of clues. Recent weather had been dry, and the deserted lot had yielded not a single fresh footprint.

They were at a dead end.

Their best theory was that her attack had been related to the WPVI and KYW attacks. Somewhere out there, someone had decided to randomly attack reporters. Her attack had been more violent than the first two, and the police were worried the suspect's efforts were escalating.

Even though her station manager had insisted she take a leave of absence, her first instinct was to get back to work, to cover the investigation herself. Being driven was her standard mode of operation, but if she had to take time off, she wouldn't waste it. Quite the opposite.

Her time away from the newsroom would allow her to pursue the details of Ally Alexander's adoption without attracting the attention of her naturally curious coworkers.

The opportunity was perfect.

She was partway through a fresh review of

the folder of news articles about her sister's fatal fire when the doorbell rang.

Sophie slid her feet into her slippers and drew the tie on her robe snug around her waist. The doorbell chimed a second time before she made it to the top of the stairs.

"Patience," she muttered, wondering if someone had sent her flowers. The doorbell chimed once more. If so, the delivery guy could use a little yoga or something.

Her stomach tightened when she peeked through the peephole and spotted Gary waiting outside, impatience plastered across his tense features.

She yanked open her front door and shot him her on-screen smile. "To what do I owe this pleasure?"

"Save the charm for your fans."

He pushed past her without waiting for an invitation.

Sophie glared at his back as he headed down the hall toward her kitchen. "Just make yourself at home."

"Thanks, I will. I could really use a drink."

Gary's head was already buried in her refrigerator by the time she reached the kitchen. He straightened, gripping a soda can in one hand.

She lifted a brow. "Anything else I can get you?"

"A glass would be nice."

Even if they hadn't shared a history, she would have recognized the mix of sarcasm and anger in his voice. She crossed to a row of cabinets and reached for a glass. "Is there a reason for this intrusion?"

Gary shot her a look of disbelief as he popped the seal on the soda. "Can't a guy check up on an old friend?"

He moved close—too close—hooking her chin with his fingers and examining her face. "How is your head, anyway?"

Heat pooled inside her, and Sophie swallowed, wanting nothing more than to move to the opposite side of the room. Instead, she stood her ground.

"I need to take it easy for a little while." She pushed his hand away from her face. "That's all."

"They make you take a leave?"

She nodded. "Two weeks."

Gary took a backward step. "Have you remembered anything more about the guy?"

The sincere look of concern on his face sparked flashes of memory from their brief romance. Sophie blinked them away.

She lifted her chin to meet his gaze, shaking her head. "A little taller than you, but very lean."

"Hair color?"

"Ski mask."

"Eyes?"

Sophie squeezed her own eyes shut and tried to remember, tried to picture the scene. Her heartbeat quickened in response. "I want to say they were light, but I can't be sure." She shook her head. "One minute I was trying to get help for Cookie, the next minute I was on the asphalt."

Gary winced. "You're lucky you weren't more seriously injured."

She gave him a weak smile, touched by the note of caring in his voice. "Thank God the police were close by."

He shifted his focus to the floor for a moment then refocused on her face, his expression having morphed from gentle to intense. "I have a message for you from Maggie and Robert."

Sophie's heart caught. "You told them?"

He nodded. "They've agreed to a DNA test if you agree to keep this entire witch hunt of yours out of the press."

Her hopes dropped. "We don't share any DNA." She set the glass down and leaned heavily against her kitchen counter, turning her back on Gary to hide her reaction.

Proving Ally's genetics could have been so simple, if only Sophie and Rebecca had been biological sisters. But they hadn't been. And Sophie had nothing of Rebecca's that might yield DNA. No hairbrushes. No old toothbrushes. Nothing.

She gave a fleeting, crazy thought to exhuming Becca's body, but the rational part of her brain knew such action would be impossible without drawing local media attention.

Sophie flashed back to the years before her sister's death, before her mother's downward spiral, to the time when their family had seemed complete. Whole. Sadness pulled at her, but she shoved it away.

When she turned around, Gary wore a look

of utter disbelief. "What in the hell is that supposed to mean?"

Sophie shrugged. "We were both adopted. We're not related by blood. If we were, then yes, testing Ally's DNA would be the logical next step, but we're not."

"You were adopted and yet you're still willing to disrupt that little girl's life?"

The same twinge of guilt that had flickered to life when Cook had made a similar point, nagged at Sophie now, but she fought against the emotion. She shouldn't feel guilty for wanting to know whether or not her niece was alive.

My God, she was only human.

She pulled herself taller, ignoring her physical pain. "Are you going to stand there and tell me your reporter's instinct doesn't want to know the truth? Are you going to tell me you could walk away right now without ever knowing if maybe…just maybe…my niece survived that fire?"

Gary nodded, the set of his jaw firm, the look in his eyes bordering on frigid. "I could. Sometimes people are more important than the story."

Sophie narrowed her eyes at him, stepped close and jabbed a finger into his chest. "Liar."

His only response was a deepening of his glare.

She spun away from him, racing into the living room where she'd left Robin's baby album. She flipped the pages and headed back down the hall to the kitchen, foisting the photo of the birthmark at Gary as she returned.

IDENTICAL.

The bottom fell out of Gary's stomach.

Not a similar birthmark. An identical birthmark.

He might as well have been looking at the back of Ally's neck.

So much for the statistics he'd found on similar marks. He'd found nothing on identical marks, but his gut told him the occurrence would more than likely have insurmountable odds.

Could she really be Robin Markham? But how?

"And if my niece did survive that fire, are you going to tell me you don't want to know how?" Sophie's sharp tone sliced into his thoughts as if she'd read his mind. "Or why? Or who was involved?"

He didn't answer, but continued to stare at the photo in the album.

"Did someone kidnap her and set the fire to cover it up?" Sophie continued, bordering on babbling now. "Did a good Samaritan stumble along in time to save Robin but not my sister? Did someone see an opportunity to pass the infant off as their own?"

Gary flipped through a few more pages, his heart aching at the sight of the smiling, happy infant. She'd been so beautiful.

He glanced up at Sophie, who gave a slight shake of her head, confidence growing in her expression. She knew she had his interest. She always had been able to read him like a book.

Damn her.

She tipped her head to one side. "Are you going to stand there and tell me you don't want to chase that story?"

When he finally answered her, he spoke slowly and flatly. "You're talking about my sister's family, Sophie, not some stranger across town who looks like a good headline."

He knew he'd pushed a button as soon as color fired in her cheeks. "Do you honestly think that's what this is about? A headline?"

"It would be an eye-catcher, wouldn't it? Local Reporter Spots Long-lost Niece at Community Leader's Fund-raiser."

She looked as though he'd slapped her. The accusation was a harsh one, but it had to be made. He had to be certain her intentions were pure. She was a reporter, after all, and had a reputation for getting the story above everything else.

If there was one thing Gary knew all too well, it was how much reporters loved an exclusive.

"I want to know if she's my family." The sharp edge had left her voice, and the corners of her eyes had turned sad. "I owe my sister that much."

Gary studied her for several long, awkward moments, then stepped across the room before he spoke. "Sorry. I was out of line, but I had to be sure."

"Your sister and her husband must think I'm a monster."

The question caught him off guard. Sophie

wasn't one to show any vulnerability, but her question smacked of the emotion.

"They said you're insane, if you want to know the truth."

Sophie bit her lip.

He pressed on. "My niece was put up for adoption by her birth mother, not some crazed person who snatched her from a fire. They love that little girl, and now you're out to prove she's not who they think she is. How do you think you'd react if someone did the same to you?"

"I'd want to know the truth."

"Well, without any DNA for comparison, I don't know how we'll do that."

They stood in silence for a moment, then Gary rubbed his chin. "How about some of your sister's things? A hairbrush, maybe?"

Sophie shook her head. "All gone in the fire, and I've got nothing from when we were younger." She pressed her lips tightly together, then spoke tentatively. "What about an exhumation?"

Gary felt his eyebrows snap together. "Are you insane?"

"It would be the quickest way to get our answer."

"And media coverage from far and wide." He shook his head. "Absolutely not. We'll find another way."

"Does this mean you're going to help me?" Her voice climbed on the last word.

Gary closed the space between them, standing so close he could see her squirm.

"I'm thinking," he answered.

"We'd need the adoption papers. I'm sure Maggie and Robert can provide us with some sort of paper trail."

He leaned closer, so close he could feel Sophie's body heat. "She didn't hear us argue, by the way, so my sister had nothing to do with your attack."

Shame washed across Sophie's face. "I was way out of line. I was grasping at straws."

"Duly noted."

Her expression grew hopeful. "So are you with me, or not?"

He pursed his lips and frowned. "I am not *with* you. I will work alongside you, though, as long as you meet the no-press condition."

Sophie's frown matched his.

"Think about it," Gary continued. "If word of this leaks out, children's services will take

Ally from her home so fast it'll make your head spin. They'll toss her into foster care until this is all figured out. Is that what you want?"

The image of his niece flashed through his mind. Smiling. Playing. Happily snuggled on Maggie's lap. He shuddered at the thought of her being removed from her family.

"No." Sophie shook her head. "We'll keep this between us. You can trust me."

"Fair enough."

Gary gestured toward her pajamas and robe, and watched a blush crawl up her neck.

He reached around her for the glass she'd plucked from the cabinet, still holding the soda can in the opposite hand.

"You'd better get dressed—" Sophie stiffened as he brushed her shoulder "—if we're going to pay my sister a visit."

IT HAD BEEN EARLY EVENING by the time Sophie and Gary reached the Alexander home, and now they all gathered in the sitting room, an awkward silence hanging in the air.

Maggie ruffled Ally's short hair. "Why don't you run to the kitchen and color a picture for Uncle Gary?"

The little girl took off like a shot, and Sophie stared after her, returning her focus to Maggie only when Gary noisily cleared his throat.

Maggie's pale eyes might as well have been shooting daggers for all of the contempt they showed. Trevor James held up both hands and spoke in an even, soothing tone. "Perhaps we should all take a moment to center ourselves before we begin."

As usual, Maggie's life coach had been planted on the sofa when Gary and Sophie had arrived. The man obviously spent more time with Maggie than he did his other clients. Hell, when did he have time for other clients?

"*We* have nothing to begin." Gary blew out an exasperated breath. "This is a family matter."

"Trevor is family," Maggie said defensively. "Anything that has to be said can be said in his presence."

Sophie and Gary exchanged a wary glance.

"I thought you were concerned about privacy?" Sophie asked Maggie.

"Trevor does not—"

Trevor James stood and placed a hand gently on Maggie's shoulder. "It's all right. I'll go check on Ally. Excuse me."

Gary waited until the man's footsteps faded down the center hall before he spoke. "The DNA testing isn't a possibility without drawing too much attention, we're going to need to see the paperwork to get this over with."

Pale pink blotches fired in Maggie's cheeks. "I don't understand."

"My sister and I were adopted." Sophie gave a tired smile. "We didn't share DNA."

"So there's no reason to compare Ally's DNA to Sophie's," Gary explained.

"You're willing to upset my child's life just to answer your curiosity?"

Gary watched the anger flash to life in Sophie's eyes, then watched as she squelched the emotion even more quickly than it had appeared.

There had been times during their brief relationship when he'd wanted to grab her shoulders and shake her until she admitted her feelings. The familiar urge nearly overcame him now. How had she survived all these years with her impenetrable walls in place? Or maybe, he realized, that was exactly how she had survived.

"If your daughter is my niece—" Sophie's

tone had grown soft, yet determined "—she's my only living relative. I have to know the truth." She leaned forward, pinning Maggie with her intense stare. "I have to understand what happened."

Maggie's eyes narrowed to angry slits, and she lowered her voice. "*My* daughter is not *your* niece."

"Then show us the paperwork to—"

Gary placed his hand on Sophie's and she fell silent. He met his sister's pained gaze. "Let's get this over with. Okay?"

His sister's eyes glistened with moisture and his heart twisted. He hated to see her like this, hated to see the fear of loss in her eyes.

"Robert keeps everything at the office." Maggie sounded defeated, her voice barely audible. "He's working late tonight. I'll tell him you're coming over."

In a matter of seconds, the two said their goodbyes and were headed back toward Gary's car. Sophie walked ahead, not giving so much as a backward glance at the house as they headed down the sidewalk.

"How do you do it?"

He took a small measure of satisfaction at

the way her steps faltered with his words. She hesitated, turning back to face him a few steps shy of reaching his car.

"Do what?"

She'd regained control of her emotionally guarded expression, and he scowled as he walked toward her, stopping mere inches from where she stood.

Gary pointed to her face. Her eyes narrowed reflexively. "That. How do you act like you don't care when I know deep down you do. Remember, I saw you tear up earlier."

Sophie visibly flinched.

"Are you that afraid of someone glimpsing the real you?"

She shrugged. "What if this is the real me?"

The move ignited the frustration that had been simmering deep inside Gary's gut. He brought his mouth down over hers, brusquely. Sophie stiffened, but he pinned her to him, wrapping one arm around her back and cupping the other to her face.

When her lips softened beneath his and her body relaxed, he broke away, rounding the trunk of his car as he pressed the key fob to release the door lock, all the while ignoring how right it had felt to hold her after all these years.

Sophie still stood where he'd left her, but turned slowly to face him, fury firing in her dark brown gaze, hot-pink circles staining her cheeks.

"What the hell was that?" To say her tone was indignant would be the understatement of the century.

He shrugged, then slid into the driver's seat.

"I deserve an answer." Sophie dropped into the passenger seat, slammed the door and crossed her arms over her chest. "I did absolutely nothing to encourage that." She jerked her thumb toward where they'd stood.

Gary twisted on the ignition, smiling to himself.

"Well?" Her voice climbed an octave or two.

"An experiment." He pressed down on the gas, easing the Mustang away from the curb.

"Experiment?"

"Just wanted to see what it would take to make that control of yours slip."

Sophie's brown eyes narrowed to slits.

He let out a soft chuckle as he pulled a U-turn, heading back toward center-city Philadelphia and Robert's office. "I'd say mission accomplished."

As they drove, the specter of their kiss hung in the silence between them. Gary didn't know what had come over him. What had he been thinking? He hadn't been thinking. That was the problem. He'd been so infuriated by how closed off she'd become that he'd acted first, regretted later.

When Sophie had walked away and never looked back seven years earlier, he'd sworn her off then and there. Hell, he'd sworn off romantic entanglements period, and he'd avoided them just fine ever since.

There was nothing wrong with devoting himself to his career, and he'd made a name for himself. Just look at the pending editor's slot in Los Angeles.

He could handle that, just as he could handle any unwanted emotions that surfaced for Sophie. He was perfectly capable of shoving them so far down they'd never have a chance to surface again.

He stole a glance at her profile, the gentle curve of her jaw, the way her short hair feathered against her cheek.

Damn straight.

He could handle anything the lady could dish out. No problem.

This time around, there would be no chance of her getting under his skin.

Gary drove around the corner toward Robert's office building and retrained his focus on the task at hand.

There was plenty of on-street parking at this time of night, and he easily slid his car into an open space. Sophie was out of the car before he could get his door open.

She might be fairly banged up, but she walked at a quick clip as she pushed through the building's revolving doors and headed straight for the visitor's registration desk.

He took his time following. After all, putting a little space between himself and Ms. Markham might be just what he needed.

Chapter Six

Sophie finished signing in with the security guard, then made a beeline toward the elevator. Heat still burned her cheeks.

How dare Gary kiss her and treat her like some science experiment. She knew him well enough to know exactly what he'd been doing—trying to get a rise out of her. Trying to get a reaction.

During the time they'd been together, he'd continually pushed against her boundaries, encouraging her to try new things, to stretch emotionally, to let go of her tight control. He hadn't accepted who she'd been then, and he apparently wasn't going to accept who she was now.

No matter. She had no plans to waste a single moment worrying about what he thought or what they might have shared had they stayed together.

She was focused on only one thing. Proving Ally Alexander was Robin.

Sophie knew it. She felt it. She believed it. Without a doubt.

She tapped her foot, wondering what on earth was taking the elevator so long as she glanced up at the bank of lights. The car hadn't budged from the ninth floor during the entire time she'd been waiting.

"They only keep one running after hours." Gary's voice sounded from just behind her.

She stiffened, drawing in a long, slow breath, working to keep from turning around and showing some real emotion. Part of her wanted to scream at him, wanted to grab the front of his denim shirt and shake him. Couldn't he see that his niece was Robin? Or was it that he didn't want to?

Instead, she shoved her frustrations even deeper inside and spoke flatly. "It's barely seven o'clock."

"Some people actually have lives to go home to." Gary moved next to her, his arm brushing against hers.

She stepped aside and one of his blond brows arched.

She ignored him.

"You know how this center-city crowd is." He gave the button another jab. "Nine to five. They'd never cut it in our world."

Sophie continued to stare at the row of lights, sighing inwardly when the elevator began a steady descent. A few moments later, the bell chimed, the doors slid open, and she and Gary stepped inside.

Sophie turned toward the front of the elevator, but Gary stood facing her, studying her face, just long enough to make her want to squirm. Thankfully, he pivoted on one heel, turning his back to her as the elevator made its ascent.

They reached the twelfth floor in no time. Gary stepped through the doors as they slid open, pressing one palm against the door edges, as if shielding Sophie from being closed in.

She shook off a surge of appreciation and brushed past him, turning toward the sign for Robert Alexander's law offices.

When they reached the hand-lettered glass entryway, the space looked like a ghost town.

Maggie had called ahead, so even though the lights had been dimmed to a night setting and the reception desk sat empty, Sophie knew the man should still be in.

A shiver wound its way down her spine, just the same. She'd never been one to be afraid of the dark—or empty spaces—but a whisper of unease simmered inside her as she stood at the entrance to the dark offices.

She could try to attribute her discontent to anxiety—to excitement—but she'd be lying. The image of her attacker loomed very large and very real in her memory, just as her sore body and bruised face provided tangible reminders with every move she made.

Sophie blinked away the unwanted sensation, recognizing it for exactly what it was. Fear.

Her stomach tilted sideways at the thought. Perhaps the first piece of the puzzle was about to fall into place. If Robert Alexander provided them with the name of the woman who had placed Ally for adoption, Sophie would be able to work backward, tracing the steps the woman had taken, looking for the tie to her niece.

Maybe, just maybe, she'd discover exactly

how and when Robin might have been removed from her home.

The voice of doubt whispered at the base of her brain. What if she was wrong? What if the adoption was perfectly legitimate—perfectly legal—and she'd raised these suspicions for no reason?

Becca's face floated through her mind's eye, and Sophie knew she was doing what her sister would have wanted her to do. She couldn't look the other way and wonder *what if* for the rest of her life. She'd spent her adult life chasing stories, chasing the truth. Why should she do anything differently now?

"This way."

Gary walked past her, his confident stride not slowing in the darkened foyer. She quickened her steps, following close behind him.

"Robert," Gary called out his brother-in-law's name but was answered by silence. He shot Sophie a quick glance. "Probably has his head buried in his case notes. Takes his job seriously."

"What type of law?"

"Specializes in family law." He rounded a corner and Sophie followed. "Here we go."

Gary picked up the pace, pulling up to a stop at the door of a brightly lit corner office. Sophie stopped behind him, expecting to see Robert Alexander hard at work.

They were greeted instead by an empty chair and a desk strewn with papers and files, as if a cyclone had blown through. The drawers to a small file cabinet had been pulled open, their contents upended. Hanging folders and sheets of paper covered most of the floor.

Gary muttered a stream of expletives, then put out an arm to block Sophie's entrance. The small hairs at the back of her neck pricked to attention just as her gaze fell to a sight that stopped her heart in her chest.

A man's loafer, just visible beyond the edge of the desk.

"Get help." Gary shot across the office, obviously having seen the same thing at the same moment. Sophie followed just behind, biting back a gasp at the sight of Robert Alexander, bloodied and battered. Unconscious.

Gary dropped to his knees, checking for a pulse, loosening his brother-in-law's tie as he barked out orders.

"Call 911. Call security. See if you can find a blanket somewhere."

Sophie froze momentarily as Gary ripped a piece of duct tape from Robert's mouth. A piece of tape identical to the one that had been used during her attack. She snapped herself out of the trance, fumbling for the phone on the desk, doing as she'd been told, while Gary assessed Robert's condition.

"They're on their way. How is—"

"Breathing's shallow, but he's breathing." Gary lifted his gaze to hers, his eyes shuttered and dark. "He's probably in shock."

Sophie didn't wait for him to say anything more. She dashed out into the hall, searching for a lounge, a closet, anything that might yield something to keep Robert warm.

She found what she needed a few doors away, a small break room with a sofa and several chairs. A chenille throw sat neatly folded over the arm of the sofa and she grabbed it, reversing her direction back toward Robert's office.

As Gary gently covered his brother-in-law and murmured words of encouragement to him, Sophie let her gaze wander around the room, doing her best to read the label on every file scattered across the desk and floor.

"The file wouldn't have been in the cabinet," Gary said, as if reading her mind.

She shouldn't have been surprised. His brain worked just as hers did, constantly analyzing situations and possibilities.

"Where then?" she asked.

Gary tipped his chin toward the desk. "Bottom drawer. He told me once that's where he kept anything personal. Use a tissue or something, don't mess up any prints."

Sophie plucked a tissue from a box on Robert's credenza and pulled at the drawer. The locking mechanism had been splintered clear out of the wood and the drawer sat empty—completely empty—any contents it had once held, gone.

She sagged with disappointment, then caught herself. How could she be so selfish when the young husband and father lay on the floor, severely beaten?

Was his attack her fault? Did someone out there know the truth and want it kept hidden? At any cost? It was too much of a coincidence to think Robert's attack could be unrelated to Ally's adoption, not with every personal file missing.

Noises and running footfalls sounded in the hall, shattering Sophie's train of thought. She stepped out of the way, moving into the hall as two police officers and a team of paramedics took over.

When Gary stepped to her side, she didn't stiffen or move away. When he wrapped an arm around her and pulled her close, she leaned into him, welcoming the solid feel of his body next to hers.

She began to tremble, as if the magnitude of the scene before her had finally sunk in. Gary pulled her closer, rubbing his hand up and down her arm. Sophie relaxed into his embrace, letting the warmth of his touch wind its way under her skin.

She could be tough again later.

For now, as her mind wondered what ghosts her investigation had resurrected from the past, her body needed Gary's comforting embrace, whether she liked it or not.

"SOMEONE WANTS THE TRUTH to stay hidden."

"Sophie, you're not thinking logically."

Gary jerked the steering wheel and careened into the hospital parking lot at Jefferson Hospital. As he navigated the sloped entrance and narrow driveway, he did his best to focus on Sophie's words. Concentration wasn't easy.

He couldn't shake the image of Robert, battered and beaten as the paramedics had rushed him away. He could only imagine what sort of emotional state Maggie must be in. His priority now was to get to his sister… and fast.

"Who knows about your suspicions? You? Me? My sister?" He shot a quick glance at Sophie as he maneuvered down another row of parked cars, searching for a space. "Do you think she did this to her own husband, or hired someone to do it for her?"

She fell silent, then slowly lifted her gaze to his. "Hundreds of thousands of people saw that interview I did with Maggie at the SIDS fund-raiser. What if someone saw the broadcast and decided he couldn't wait for us to put the pieces together? What if he decided to eliminate the risks now?"

Gary pulled the car to a stop and cut the ignition, looking up to carefully study

Sophie's expression. He'd never seen her look more serious—or more certain. And for the first time since he'd run into her at the fund-raiser, the light had returned to her eyes. Sophie looked alive.

While he'd rather her reawakening had been due to something other than his own family, he was glad to see the glimmer of the girl he once knew, nonetheless.

"Now what?" She frowned.

But Gary was already in motion. There was no time to waste. He and Sophie had been held for questioning and it had been nearly an hour since Robert had been taken by ambulance. The police had believed Robert's story about their late evening visit being nothing more than an invitation to dinner. They'd taken note of the empty file drawer, but neither Gary nor Sophie had shared their suspicion that the adoption paperwork had been among the information stolen.

If that information leaked to the police—and then to the media—Maggie, Robert and Ally would be front-page news by morning. Avoiding that was something he knew they all agreed upon.

He rounded the trunk of the car, grabbed Sophie's elbow as she climbed out of the passenger seat, and hurried her along toward a bank of elevators.

"What do we do now?" He punched the elevator button and Sophie jerked her arm free of his touch. So much for the closeness they'd shared back at the scene of the crime.

"Now we find my sister," he continued. "We see what kind of shape my brother-in-law is in, and depending on how well all that goes, we tell Maggie the paperwork vanished in the attack."

He turned to lock gazes with Sophie, hoping his expression clearly communicated the seriousness of what he was about to say. "Then, if she's up to it—and only if she's up to it—we see just how much she can remember about the woman who placed Ally for adoption."

A few moments later, they spotted Maggie, sitting alone, her face devoid of all color, her eyes looking huge and frightened.

"Where's her guru now?" Gary muttered.

"What?" Sophie's features twisted with confusion.

"Nothing." He shook his head, deciding

he didn't need to share his dislike of Trevor James with Sophie.

Tears slid down Maggie's cheeks as their eyes met, and Gary bundled his older sister into his arms.

"He'll be all right," he spoke softly against her hair. "You'll see. He had one heck of a pulse back there. He's a fighter."

He held her out to arm's length and swiped away her tears with a brush of his knuckles against her cheeks. Sophie stood awkwardly to the side, looking as if she weren't sure she should be there at all.

Maggie turned to face her, pasting on her social-function smile. "Thanks for coming."

Sophie nodded, pressed her fingertips lightly to Maggie's arm then dropped her hand to her side.

"Any word from the doctor?" Gary asked.

Maggie shook her head.

He helped her back into her seat, then sat close beside her, wrapping her hands inside his own.

"Can I get you anything?" Sophie asked, her expression painted with a jumble of emotions Gary couldn't quite sort out.

"Coffee," he answered. "Sound good, Mag?"

His sister nodded. Sophie turned on her heel and was gone.

Gary brushed a wayward strand of blond hair from Maggie's damp cheek, tucking it behind her ear. "Where's Ally?"

"At a neighbor's. I didn't tell her what happened." She gazed at him wide-eyed, looking a good fifteen years younger than her age. "Was that wrong?"

Gary shook his head, then pressed a kiss to her forehead. "That was perfect. You did the absolute right thing."

"Why would anyone do this to Robert?"

He gave his head another quick shake. "I don't know. But the police will find out. They were swarming the building."

"He's a good man," Maggie said softly and Gary's heart twisted inside his chest.

He couldn't bear to see her endure the loss of Robert. He could only pray they'd found him and gotten him help quickly enough.

Sophie had no sooner returned with three cups of coffee than a doctor emerged from the triage area and squatted in front of Maggie.

"I expect him to make a full recovery, Mrs. Alexander."

Gary felt his sister sag with relief.

"He'll be in the hospital for a while, and it's necessary right now to keep him in a medically induced coma, but he's got strong vitals."

"Coma?" The word was barely audible, Maggie uttered it so softly.

The doctor nodded, offering a reassuring smile before he continued. "He's got a punctured lung and some significant injuries. Because of that, he's on a respirator. He's heavily sedated so he won't fight the breathing tube. We want to give his body time to heal."

Punctured lung. Breathing tube.

The magnitude of his brother-in-law's injuries struck Gary full-force. He'd do whatever he could to expose whoever had done this.

"You don't need to stay with me," Maggie said flatly a few moments after the doctor walked away. "I'll be all right."

Emotional exhaustion tinged her words, and Gary reached over to give her knee a quick squeeze. "I'm not going anywhere."

Sophie stood, smoothing the front of her

slacks. "I'm going to give you two some privacy. I'll catch a cab home."

Maggie blinked. "After what you've just been through. No." She straightened, as if determination to see Sophie home safely had bolstered her energy reserves. "Gary can take you. I'll be fine."

Gary narrowed his eyes first at Maggie, then at Sophie. His sister never ceased to amaze him. Sophie had tipped their blissful existence on its ear, and here she was, worried about the woman getting home safely.

She tilted her head toward the elevator. "Go on."

"If I go, I'm coming right back."

His sister gave him a weak smile. "I'm not going anywhere."

He stood, taking a step toward the elevator. Sophie's feet, however, were planted next to Maggie. She shot him a glare and raised her brows.

The file.

He'd promised her he'd ask Maggie about the adoption file if he felt she was up to it.

He took a backward step and placed a hand on his sister's shoulder. "Listen, if you're not up to this, just tell me, but I need to ask you if you've got any of Ally's adoption papers at home."

Maggie blinked, then frowned. "I told you before. They're all at Robert's office."

Gary shook his head. "Whoever attacked him emptied his personal file drawer."

Maggie inhaled sharply and placed a hand to her chest. "But why? Who?"

Gary dropped to a squat and grasped her knees. "They wanted something he had."

"The adoption papers?" A shadow slid across Maggie's exhausted features, but she mustered the energy to scowl at Sophie. "You. This is all because of you."

So much for worrying about Sophie's safety.

Gary cupped his sister's chin in his fingers and directed her attention back to him. "Think hard. Do you remember anything about the adoption? Any names?"

Tears welled again in Maggie's eyes. "I didn't want to know."

Disappointment wound its way through Gary's insides. "So, you've got nothing at home?"

Maggie shook her head. "I only wanted Ally."

"Anyone else involved? Think, Maggie. Someone did this to Robert for a reason—can you think of any reason why?"

She shook her head again. "I can't."

He didn't want to frighten his sister any more than she already was, but his next words had to be voiced out loud. "If what happened tonight is related to the adoption, you might be in danger."

Maggie's startled focus snapped into place. "Is Ally in danger?"

Gary hesitated before he answered. "I don't know."

His sister shot another angry glare at Sophie, who had taken a few steps toward the elevator, apparently wanting a little distance between herself and Maggie's wrath.

"Brian Franklin."

His sister's exhausted voice jolted his attention away from Sophie.

"Judge Franklin?" Sophie straightened, unmasked curiosity flashing across her features.

Maggie nodded, and Gary dropped his hand back to her knee.

"He used to be Robert's partner. Way back when they both started out. He helped us with the adoption." Her tone dropped low. "He pushed through…everything."

Gary's pulse quickened. "Are you saying you didn't follow normal channels?"

Maggie lifted her gaze to his, tears swimming in her eyes. "I don't know. I just know Robert did whatever it took to make that precious baby girl our own."

Brian Franklin. The outspoken district circuit judge now up for the New Jersey Supreme Court. He had a motive to keep an illegally orchestrated adoption quiet, if anyone did. But was he capable of such a violent attack on Robert?

Gary stole a glance at Sophie and determination blazed in her eyes, the unspoken thought understood in the silence between them.

They had a new piece of the puzzle to pursue.

"There's more." Maggie's voice had grown distant, as if she'd give anything to be somewhere else. "Her name was Teresa Cartwright."

"The birth mother?" Gary asked.

Maggie nodded. "She was from somewhere in northwestern Pennsylvania."

"I thought you didn't know any of this?" Sophie asked.

Gary shot her a warning glance, but the look in her eyes remained hard, unwavering.

Maggie looked at the floor, her voice barely more than a whisper. "I know the name of the woman who made my dream come true."

A few moments later, they'd left Maggie behind. The elevator jerked to a stop when they reached the floor where Gary had parked the Mustang.

When the doors slid open, Sophie hesitated just outside.

Gary worked to keep his anger with Sophie at bay, but he couldn't. Her last remark had been totally unnecessary.

"You had no right to say that back there."

She spun on him. "What if she took part in an illegal adoption? What if Teresa Cartwright wasn't even the baby's mother? What if they never checked?" Color fired in her cheeks. "I had every right to say that."

They stood in silence for several awkward moments, staring at each other. Each too stubborn to be the first one to speak or make a move.

Finally, Sophie squinted at him, tipping her chin up to look him squarely in the face. "The attacker used the same tape."

Now it was Gary's turn to squint. "What tape?"

"The duct tape you ripped from Robert's mouth when we found him."

He shook his head, his mind whirling with a jumble of possibilities, but too tired to make sense of any of them. "I'm not following you."

"It was the same tape my attacker used on me."

He studied her without saying a word. The bandage over her eye. The bruised cheek. The split lip.

Could the attacks have been related? Was Sophie right? Had someone decided to eliminate any evidence tied to Ally's adoption before a connection to Robin Markham could be made?

"It was the same tape," Sophie repeated. "Same tape. Same attacker."

"Anyone can buy duct tape," he countered. She shook her head, then turned toward the car. "I don't believe in coincidences. If Brian Franklin is behind Robert's attack, my money says he was behind mine as well."

Gary stood for a moment watching her walk away, letting her words bounce through his brain.

I don't believe in coincidences.

Funny thing was, neither did he.

Chapter Seven

Sophie's heart tattooed against her ribs as she hurried across the hospital parking lot the next morning. Cook had regained consciousness and was coherent. Cookie's wife had called her with the good news.

She'd put a quick call in to Gary, and they'd agreed to meet a bit later that morning to pay a visit to Brian Franklin.

Sophie stopped at the nurses' desk to make sure visitors were allowed. When the nurse gave her the go-ahead, she hurried down the hall, the heels of her pumps clicking against the linoleum floor. When she rounded the corner into Cook's room, relief surged through her.

Cook sat upright in bed, battered and bruised, but smiling. His wife clasped his hand and the two spoke softly to one another.

A pang of guilt sliced through Sophie. Maybe she shouldn't be here now asking questions. Perhaps she should let the two have some time alone—time to celebrate Cook's recovery.

Sophie hesitated, admiring the joy painted across both Cook's and Anne's faces. True love. Something she'd probably never know. Regret tapped at the base of her brain, but she shoved it away. Far, far away.

Before she could back out of the doorway, Cook's attention shifted in her direction.

"Well, look who it is. Do you sleep in those suits of yours?"

Sophie glanced down at today's suit, a vivid green that she knew set off her dark hair and eyes. It was probably crazy to dress so formally while she was out on leave, but old habits died hard. She'd worn a suit for as long as she could remember. Reaching into her closet each morning had become a habit.

She walked toward the bed, rolling her eyes at the man. "Hey, some of us have a reputation to keep up. You don't see me loafing around in some hospital bed."

Anne stood, giving Cook a quick peck on

the forehead. She squeezed Sophie's hand as she moved to leave. "I'll give you two some privacy. I know John wants to talk to you."

Sophie watched the woman leave, turning to face Cook when he cleared his throat. "Are you in a lot of pain?" The guilt in her gut spread outward, reaching up, threatening to choke her.

Had the attack been her fault? What if she really was to blame for Cook's injuries?

He winked, and she smiled. When he patted the edge of the bed, she sat down carefully, then reached out to touch his cheek. "You scared me."

He nodded. "I'm a tough old guy. Gonna take a lot more than a broken rib or two to keep me down."

She swallowed down the lump in her throat, dropping her focus to her lap.

"How about you?" Cook asked. "Don't think we've got enough makeup to cover those bruises. I heard about what happened. You sure you're all right?"

Sophie met his worried gaze with a smile. "I'm a tough old broad. I learned from the best."

They sat in companionable silence for several moments, then Sophie asked the question she had no doubt Cook had already thought through.

"Did you see anything? Get a look at him before he hit you?"

"Happened fast." His voice dropped low, and his features grew serious. "I was packing up when he came up beside me."

"So you couldn't see anything?" Disappointment flickered through her.

"Didn't say that."

She narrowed her gaze, frowning at the man.

"I saw his boots."

"Boots?"

"Black." Cook's brows furrowed. "Combat boots. Work boots. You know the type." He nodded. "Black," he repeated.

Sophie forced a weak smile. "Doesn't really narrow it down, does it?"

"It was the damnedest thing." He shook his head.

Sophie straightened, sudden anticipation kicking to life in her belly. "What?"

"The toes were spattered with paint. White paint."

Sophie lifted her brows, working to process the information.

Cook reached out and took her hand, giving it a quick squeeze. "One section of droplets looked like a smiley face." He chuckled, his tone bitter and disbelieving. "A damned smiley face. I was about to get beaten within an inch of my life, and there I was staring at the guy's feet."

Sophie patted his hand, her mind racing through the possibilities. It wasn't much, but it was something.

And something was a whole lot better than the nothing they'd had to go on so far.

GARY RUBBED A HAND ACROSS his exhausted face and hit the Delete key. Again. No matter how hard he tried, he couldn't wrap his brain around the article he had due the next day.

Normally, nothing could distract him from his job or a deadline, but spending the night with Maggie at the hospital hadn't done much for his ability to concentrate.

Robert's condition had stabilized overnight and they were hopeful he'd be able to breathe on his own before too long. Gary had taken

Maggie home to let her clean up and rest a bit, promising to meet her at the hospital later on.

He hit the Save key and closed his file, knowing he wasn't getting anywhere today. He'd use his free time before his planned meeting with Sophie to do some additional digging on Robert's attack.

As much as he hated to admit it, the long night at the hospital wasn't the only thing wreaking havoc on his brain. Ever since Sophie had waltzed back into his life, her face remained planted in his mind's eye.

Sure, it was probably because she'd made it her personal campaign to prove his niece was her niece, but his gut knew differently. His gut knew being near her was slowly eroding his self-control.

Sophie Markham had burned him once in the romance department. He sure as hell wasn't going to set himself up to get burned again. Yet the kiss they'd shared the day before lingered in his mind. Even worse, anytime he let himself think about the feel of her lips against his, his traitorous stomach twisted into a tight knot.

"Earth to Barksdale."

Randy Simpson's voice jolted Gary back to reality and he looked up. "What's up?"

The crime reporter slid a sheet of paper onto Gary's desk. "Thought you might be interested."

Gary studied the list of names, frowning. "What is it?"

"List of visitors at your brother-in-law's building yesterday. Buddy on the force slipped it to me."

Gary had to hand it to Simpson. The man's contacts were the stuff of legends.

"Skip to the bottom." Simpson's voice held an emotion Gary hadn't heard there in years. Excitement.

Gary glanced up then back to the paper, skimming the names toward the bottom of the sheet until he saw it.

"I'll be damned."

Simpson slapped the desk then walked away. "Thought you'd like that," he called out over his shoulder as he walked away.

Gary stared at the paper, unable to wrench his eyes from the name.

Trevor James.

He checked the clock on his desk as he

reached for his car keys. Assuming the life coach extraordinaire was in his office, Gary had just enough time to pay him a visit before he met Sophie.

FIVE MINUTES INTO his conversation with Trevor James, Gary found himself fighting the urge to slap the smirk off the man's face.

Each strand of hair fell impeccably into place on James's head. He maintained such an emotionless expression that Gary wouldn't have been surprised if James himself told him he'd updated every facial feature through plastic surgery.

How could someone so unwilling to show his own feelings inspire others to reach for the stars?

"I have several clients in that building," James offered by way of explanation. "I had every right to be there."

The man leaned back in his cushy leather chair, the Philadelphia skyline gleaming behind the windows of his massive corner office.

The guru business must be treating him very well.

Gary reined in his dislike for the man and

shifted his focus to uncovering why James had been at Robert's building shortly before he and Sophie had arrived.

"Clients such as whom?"

Gary mirrored James's relaxed stance, leaning back against his chair. He bit back his own smirk when James kicked his feet up onto the desk. The man might as well have a sign posted proclaiming his superiority to all those who might visit.

"I'm afraid not all of my clients like their use of my methods broadcast to the world." James offered a slight shrug as means of explanation. "I often check in with them after hours, when the office halls are less traveled, so to speak."

"Have you heard about Robert's attack?"

James nodded. "Maggie called me as soon as it happened."

Naturally, Gary thought. The hold this man possessed over his sister never ceased to amaze him.

"So who were you visiting?"

One of James's brows lifted. "My clients prefer their privacy, Gary. I'm sure you understand."

Gary leaned forward, his dislike for the man morphing into a simmering anger, gnawing at the lining of his stomach. "I'd bet the police didn't accept that answer."

James pursed his lips and Gary mentally cringed at the smug expression.

"No," Trevor answered. "They didn't. But they assured me my answers would be kept confidential. Considering your position with the newspaper, I can't say I'd trust you to do the same."

Gary stood, leaning over the man's desk. "How about for Maggie? I'd think you'd offer up a name or two if it might help the investigation."

James did not stand to meet Gary's gaze. In fact, he picked up the phone and dialed, dismissing Gary with the simple movement.

"Why would my business help the investigation?" His tone had dropped low, annoyed.

Gary smiled at the crack in the man's flawless persona.

"What if you had something to do with the attack?"

That got James's attention. His cold gaze lifted to Gary's as he spoke. "I'm not going to dignify that with an answer. If you'll excuse me, I've got clients to call."

"I'm sure you do," Gary said as he turned toward the door. "I'll see myself out."

"Good luck with your investigation." James's tone had shifted to one of superiority once more. "Call me if you'd ever like to set some career goals that might move you beyond simple reporting."

Gary bristled at the remark, but chose not to reply, heading into the hall and toward the elevator instead. Once inside, he slammed his fist against the doors as they closed.

James might have nothing to do with Robert's attack, but something about the man didn't sit right. One of these days, Gary was going to figure out exactly what that was.

Then he was going to use his *simple reporting* to expose the man for all of Philadelphia to see.

A SHORT WHILE LATER, HE SAT at the Penn Queen diner waiting for Sophie to show up. When her sleek sedan slid into a parking space and she hurriedly climbed out, he shook his head.

Another damned suit, this one a rich green. He had to admit the getup did great things for her legs, not to mention her curves, but hadn't the woman ever heard of casual dress? She was on leave, for crying out loud.

"How's Cook?" he asked as she slid into the booth.

She smiled, lines of exhaustion winking through the yellowing bruises on her face. "I think he's going to be all right."

"Does he remember anything?" Gary gestured to a passing waitress and pointed to Sophie's empty coffee cup.

Sophie sat back against the padded seat and raised her dark brows. "A smiley face."

Gary frowned and curiosity bubbled to life inside him. "A smiley face?"

She fell silent as the waitress approached, filled her cup, topped off Gary's, then left.

Sophie popped open a packet of cream, poured it into her cup, then refocused on Gary.

"On the attacker's boot, to be more specific," she continued.

Gary continued to frown at her. "You might want to explain that a bit better to me."

A smile tugged at the corner of Sophie's

lips, but vanished as soon as it appeared. "The only thing Cook saw before he was knocked unconscious were his attacker's boots. They had paint spatter over the toes, and the only thing Cook remembers is a smiley face."

She gave a quick lift and drop of her shoulders.

"In the paint?" Gary asked. Now, he'd heard it all.

Sophie nodded, pressing her lips into a wry smile.

"What kind of boots?"

She held up a finger as she took a long sip of coffee, answering after she'd swallowed. "Black. Military maybe."

"Doesn't give us much to go on." Gary pulled out his wallet, extracted enough cash to pay for their two coffees and slid the bills under the sugar dish.

Sophie shook her head. "Maybe not, but at least it's something."

Gary slid out of the booth, standing next to the table. "Drink up. Maybe our visit to Judge Franklin will provide even more information."

Sophie pushed her coffee cup away,

grabbed her purse and stood next to him. "Let's go."

He pressed his hand to her back as they stepped outside, dropping his touch once he realized what he'd done. Warmth spread up his arm, and he mentally chastised himself.

Distance. He needed to keep his distance from Sophie and his memory of how things had once been between them.

His only goal was to keep an eye on her and use her for assistance in getting to the truth about Ally's adoption. Nothing more.

She turned to face him, and he couldn't help but notice the flush of color in her cheeks. Perhaps the quick brush of his hand against her back had sent her thoughts down the same path.

"So how was your morning?" she asked. "Any news on Robert's attack?"

He nodded as he opened the driver's door of his Mustang. "I'll fill you in on my visit to Trevor James on our way into town."

"TREVOR JAMES?" Surprise washed across Sophie as she settled in the passenger seat of Gary's car. Not only surprise that Gary had gone to see Trevor James, but also surprise at the way her body had responded to Gary's brief touch.

Her insides had done a quick somersault and hadn't quite settled down yet. She'd have to do a better job at keeping her emotions in check. Typically, maintaining her cool exterior wasn't difficult. Of course, she wasn't typically working alongside Gary. The man had a definite impact on her self-control, and that was exactly what she didn't need.

She needed to keep her eye on the prize— ascertaining Ally's true identity. If she let her heart and emotions get involved with Gary, she'd have a hard time taking action against his sister and brother-in-law once she had proof Ally was Robin.

And she would take action. Shared history, or no shared history.

Sophie pressed a hand against her stomach, willing her insides to settle down. "Why Trevor James?"

"He was on the visitor's registry at Robert's building. Late in the day. Not long before you and I jotted down our names."

He eased the car to a stop at the parking-lot exit and shot her a glance. "Matter of fact, I'm surprised neither you nor I spotted his name."

Sophie narrowed her gaze, nodding. Truth was, she wasn't entirely surprised. Her only thought at the time had been how angry Gary had made her feel by kissing her.

There it was again. Distraction.

She shook her head and blew out a frustrated breath. She had phenomenal attention to detail and normally would have never missed spotting James's name.

"Problem?" Gary's voice tightened with concern.

She shot him a forced smile. "Just can't believe we didn't see it. Did he tell you why he'd been there?"

Gary nodded. "Some secret client meeting, apparently. Basically, I got nothing out of questioning him."

Excitement began to flicker to life inside Sophie's chest. "Do you think he attacked Robert?"

Gary pulled the car onto Route 130, heading for downtown Camden. He scowled. "Probably not. I just don't like the guy."

"No kidding." She chuckled and glanced out the window.

"That obvious?"

"Let's just say I wouldn't take up poker, if I were you."

Sophie warmed at the easy banter, losing herself for a second to the witty repartee they'd once enjoyed. She shook herself back to reality a moment later, shoving the past back where it belonged. Into the past.

"Listen, I think we need to be direct with Franklin."

The serious tone of Gary's voice was exactly what she needed to redirect her thoughts to the task at hand—their unannounced visit to Judge Brian Franklin.

"Tell him straight out we know he was partners with Robert at the time of the adoption?"

Gary nodded. "Exactly. He isn't going to like it, but if he was involved in fast-tracking adoption finalization papers without the necessary waiting period and clearances, I'm guessing we'll be able to read the guilt on his face."

Sophie made a snapping noise with her

mouth. "I wouldn't be too sure. The man's got everything to lose. If this came out, I'm guessing his appointment to the New Jersey Supreme Court would instantly vanish."

"Nice motive for giving Robert a warning and stealing evidence, don't you think?"

"Definitely."

As Gary made the turn toward the Hall of Justice, a swarm of news vans captured Sophie's attention.

"Big trial we don't know about?" Gary asked.

"Hardly." But Sophie frowned, her gut telling her some big story had broken and both of them had missed word of the development. "I see a WNJZ van. I'll find out what's going on."

But as Gary eased the car to a stop, his cell phone buzzed, and he held up a finger, gesturing for her to wait. She did so, concentrating solely on the expression that played across Gary's features as he listened to his caller.

He disconnected and blew out a short breath.

"What?"

"We can forget about our visit to Franklin."

"Why?"

"It just hit the wires." He slipped the phone back into his pocket. "He's dead."

Sophie's heart dropped. "Dead?"

"Fishing accident." Gary put the car into reverse and maneuvered away from the crowd. "Couple of kids found his body this morning up in the Poconos."

"What on earth was he doing in the Poconos?" Disbelief rushed through her.

"Annual retreat."

Her pulse quickened. "So anyone who knew him would know he'd be there?"

Gary nodded, determination bright in his eyes. "My thoughts exactly."

Sophie glanced back toward the bedlam outside the courthouse as they drove away. Her mind raced through the possibilities. Was someone trying to methodically destroy evidence before they could get to it?

She gave herself a mental shake. She knew better than to jump to a conspiracy theory. The man had been fishing, for God's sake. People did have accidents.

But still, a strong flicker of doubt lingered at the base of her brain.

Gary masterfully pulled the car out into

traffic. "We'll leave the Franklin investigation to the police. At least we've got another name to chase."

Comprehension eased through Sophie. "Teresa Cartwright."

The corner of Gary's mouth curved into a determined smile. "If we hurry, maybe we'll find her before someone else does."

Chapter Eight

They worked late into the night, each exhausting every contact they had. Just before midnight, the list of Teresa Cartwrights from Pennsylvania sat in the middle of Sophie's kitchen table.

"More coffee?" Sophie asked as she pushed away from the table and moved toward the counter.

Gary had rolled up the sleeves of his denim shirt and his hair stood on end, having been shoved back more times than she could count.

She smiled, remembering the habit from college. She'd seen him run a hand through his hair the night he'd first asked her out, during an exam, and then when she'd broken up with him. Her heart twisted.

Had it really been seven years?

"Soph?"

She shook herself from her memories. "What?"

"I said yes." His vivid gaze narrowed.

"Yes, what?" She'd kicked off her shoes hours earlier and now stood on the cool kitchen floor in her stocking feet. Her jacket hung neatly over the back of a chair, but she grimaced when she realized one tail of her silk blouse had come untucked.

"What?" She fumbled with her shirt, shoving the soft fabric back into her waistband.

A smile played at Gary's lips. "Coffee. You asked if I wanted coffee."

She groaned. Was she so tired she'd forgotten her own question?

Gary nodded toward her outfit. "Seriously, is there any reason why you haven't changed into something more comfortable? There aren't any cameras here, you know."

She felt heat rise in her cheeks. "Just habit. I usually change right from this into sweats. I didn't think it appropriate for me to slouch around in—"

"I've seen you naked."

His blunt statement stopped her mid-sentence, and she swallowed down the sudden lump in her throat.

Gary shrugged, looking as though he enjoyed calling attention to her uptight wardrobe.

"I'm just saying you can wear whatever you like around me." He tapped a finger against the sheet of paper. "How about I put on the coffee, and you tell me what you think of these names."

Sophie wanted to think herself capable of some stinging comeback to his naked remark, but when her brain didn't offer any suggestions, she slid into a chair instead, reaching for the list. "Fair enough."

A few minutes later, they had their choices narrowed down to two. The rest had been either too old or too young to be the right woman.

Sophie took a sip of the hot coffee Gary had poured and glanced at the clock. "It's too late to make phone calls. What do you think? Can you access the *Inquirer's* database?"

He nodded and keyed his name and password into a screen he'd pulled up on her laptop. One of the benefits of both of their jobs was the ability to tap into information anywhere they could find an Internet connection.

The laptop on her kitchen table worked just as well as any back at the *Inquirer* offices.

"You do know the woman could have vanished in five years." He spoke flatly as he worked the keyboard.

Sophie nodded, wrapping her hands around her coffee mug, fervently hoping their Teresa Cartwright had not left the state.

"We may as well look at this together." Gary pulled an empty chair flush against his own and patted the seat. "Two sets of eyes are always better than one."

Sophie hesitated for a split second, then moved to the spot next to him, her arm brushing against his. She ignored the sideways tilt her stomach took and focused on the laptop screen instead.

"Can't seem to get a phone number for the one," Gary muttered, his brows furrowed in concentration.

She studied his profile. The strong line of his jaw. The way his hair curled ever so slightly against his ear. She remembered how wonderful it had been to wake up to that profile way back when. She allowed herself to think about how it might be to wake up to that profile again.

Sophie winced as if someone had slapped her. She had to stop doing this. Everyone she loved died. It was that simple. She was far better off staying alone.

For good.

"What about the other one?" she said, forcing the words through her unwanted fog of emotion.

He sighed and shook his head. "Appears she was involved in robbing a chain of gas stations seven years ago. Been serving time ever since."

"Wonderful," she muttered. "You can't find anything on the other?"

"Hang on."

The sound of his keystrokes filled the quiet of the kitchen. Sophie grabbed his half-empty cup and hers and headed back toward the coffeepot to top them off.

"Damn."

The sharp, disappointed tone of Gary's voice stopped her cold. "What?"

She turned to face him. He shook his head,

lifting his gaze to hers. Disbelief shone blatant in his eyes.

"She's dead."

Sophie blinked. "When? Recently?"

"No." Gary refocused on the screen and shook his head. "That's just it. She died five years ago. Probably about a month after Maggie and Robert adopted Ally."

Sophie crossed to the kitchen table and leaned her weight against a chair. "How?"

"That's the thing, Soph."

The concern in his tone wrapped around her heart and squeezed. He stood and faced her, fine lines edging the corners of his serious eyes.

"They say it was careless smoking," Gary continued.

Sophie's heart began to race.

"She died in a house fire."

"Just like Becca." Tears suddenly blurred her vision, but she made no move to blink them away. "Where?"

"Bradston."

Where Becca had lived until just before her fateful move back home.

Sophie sagged, and Gary gripped her elbow.

"You're on to something, Soph. It's too much of a coincidence for this not to be related."

His features fell slack, defeated, and Sophie realized Gary had bought into her theory. How could he not? He was trained, just as she was, to pay attention to the evidence. To build a case.

The evidence pointed to the one thing Gary hadn't wanted to admit.

Something evil had happened the night Becca had died, and somehow…somehow, Robin had survived.

The sadness and grief she'd kept bottled inside for five years clawed at Sophie's chest, doing their best to break free. She tried to wrap her brain around the implication of Gary's words, but she couldn't. She wouldn't. But she had to.

A sense of certainty rushed through her, shoving the grief aside, replacing it with raw, urgent determination.

There was a very real possibility Becca hadn't been careless and her death hadn't been an accident.

"How fast can we make it to Bradston?" she asked.

Gary's eyes lit with understanding. "Seven hours."

Sophie broke away from Gary's touch and stepped toward the hall. "I'll be ready to go in ten minutes."

She climbed the steps slowly at first, then broke into a jog, taking the stairs as fast as she could.

If someone had murdered her sister and kidnapped her niece, she'd do whatever it took to find out who. And why.

She owed that much to her sister's memory and to the little girl she was certain was Robin.

GARY COULD ONLY THINK two things late the next morning as he and Sophie sat in Sheriff Harlan Winston's office. One, they were a long way from home. Two, they probably would have had more luck digging for information on their own.

But Sophie had wanted to make their presence known. She'd wanted to make a grand entrance and have some "face time," as she'd called it, with the local police department.

"Thanks for seeing us," he said as he slid into an uncomfortable folding chair.

Gary had to admit he'd derived a small bit of pleasure from the shocked look on her face when they'd been told the town had a police department of one. And they were looking at him.

Impatience battled with disbelief as Gary took stock of the man. Winston chewed on a toothpick and had one short sleeve rolled up over a pack of cigarettes.

Sophie and today's deep red suit stood out like a sore thumb in the no-frills office. Gary glanced down at his outfit—the same clothes he'd been in for over a day and a half now. He'd shown her up in the appropriate dress department, and the point obviously wasn't lost on the woman.

She sat on the edge of her chair as if someone had stuck a hot poker in her back.

Television reporters. They were a breed unto themselves.

This particular television reporter had wormed her way under his skin again, whether he wanted her there or not. When she'd burst into tears the night before, he'd wanted nothing more than to hold her, comfort her, protect her.

But that was neither here nor there. He'd

had a message from Los Angeles when he'd checked his voice mail. The editor's job was his if he wanted it.

Now all he had to do was give them his answer.

He stole another glance at Sophie as she sat patiently listening to Winston's diatribe about small-town politics and history.

If he took the job, he'd probably never see her again. She'd made it clear a long time ago that that was what she wanted. But he couldn't help but wonder if she'd choose differently now.

He swore silently. What a fool he was.

He'd finally gotten a job offer worthy of his experience, and here he sat, weighing his attraction to Sophie Markham against a cross-country move.

Fool.

Never mind the fact his niece apparently had been illegally adopted and perhaps kidnapped. He should be focused on protecting Maggie and Robert from any attempt to remove Ally from their home. That's what he should be worrying about.

"We were wondering if you could tell us a

bit more about Teresa Cartwright and how she died?"

Sophie's words sliced into his thoughts. Apparently, Winston had paused to take a breath and she'd jumped into the void.

Winston shifted his toothpick from one side of his mouth to the other. "Careless smoking as best we could tell. Started in the bedroom." The man shook his head. "Probably smoking in bed."

Sadness etched the corners of Sophie's eyes, but she straightened her features into her on-camera face.

Gary knew what she was thinking. Smoking in bed. Another similarity to the fire that had taken her sister's life.

"Did she leave any family, Sheriff Winston?" Sophie's smile spread wide and bright, and the move hit its desired mark.

Winston took the toothpick from his mouth and straightened in his chair, returning Sophie's smile. "No family at all, ma'am. Never even saw her around town much."

"I don't suppose an autopsy was done." Gary softened his stance, trying to adopt a nonthreatening pose.

Winston stiffened and put the toothpick back between his teeth. "No reason to. We might be small time around here compared to Philadelphia, but we know an accidental death when we see one."

"Well—" Sophie extended her hand as she stood "—we're very grateful for your time. I hope you won't mind if we stay in town for a little bit and poke around."

The sheriff hesitated, but then shook his head as he took Sophie's hand. "Won't mind at all."

Gary stood and gave the sheriff's hand a quick pump. As he and Sophie neared the office door, he hesitated and turned back, thinking of the money his sister and brother-in-law had paid to cover the supposed medical costs incurred by Cartwright.

"I don't suppose she left any inheritance? Any cash unclaimed?"

The sheriff's only response was a deep belly laugh. "That girl didn't have two nickels to rub together. She lived simple."

"Thanks."

But Gary's mind didn't accept that answer. As they said their goodbyes to Winston's secretary, he couldn't shake the doubt growing inside him.

He knew for a fact Maggie and Robert had paid the woman $25,000. Where was the money? If Cartwright had spent the cash, surely she'd have left behind something to show for it.

Otherwise, there was a tidy sum sitting in a bank account somewhere.

"I'm going to head back to the room and make some calls." He turned toward their hotel.

If he hurried, he could catch Simpson back at the paper before the man headed out to lunch. If anyone could get a trace on that cash, it would be him.

The day had turned cloudy and cool, the air holding a distinct chill from being so close to Lake Erie.

Sophie tipped her head toward a small café across the street. "I've got a sudden craving for coffee…and conversation."

"Happy hunting."

SOPHIE ENGAGED THE WAITRESS in a conversation about the weather until the other woman's curiosity got the best of her.

"So what are you doing all the way up here from Philadelphia?" the older woman asked.

She had a beautiful face, showing only faint lines. On looks alone, Sophie would have guessed her to be mid-forties, no older, yet her voice told another story.

The woman had a voice of someone who had been around the block a time or two.

Exactly the sort of local who could help Sophie do some digging into the past.

"I was trying to find an old friend of mine, but I found out she died a while back." Sophie shook her head and blinked her eyes, hoping the woman might think she was on the verge of tears. "Just awful."

The waitress leaned over the table. "Who, hon?"

Sophie looked up at her and offered a weak smile. "Teresa Cartwright."

The woman's brows lifted. "Now how on earth would you know her?"

"Our families go way back. Fathers were childhood friends." Sophie rubbed a hand across her eyes. "I just can't believe she's gone."

The waitress's expression softened and she

shook her head. "Poor thing had just announced her engagement. Said she'd just come into some money." She planted one fist on her hip. "Life can be cruel."

She'd just come into some money.

Sophie's pulse quickened, thinking of the adoption fee Maggie and Robert must have paid. Perhaps this Teresa Cartwright was the right woman, after all.

"I didn't know she had any money." Sophie frowned.

The waitress nodded, a sly look sliding across her face. She glanced to her left, then to her right, then dropped her voice low. "I heard it was some sort of deal she set up down your way. No idea what. Just that she'd come into a lot of cash."

Sophie leaned against the back of the booth. "No kidding?"

The waitress dropped her voice softer still. "Matter of fact, after the fire, folks around here wondered if someone had stolen her riches and set the fire to cover it all up."

Sophie bit the inside of her lip to keep herself from overreacting. "Was it a lot of money?" She dropped her voice to match her new friend's.

"Thousands." The waitress mouthed the word.

The adoption fee from the Alexanders, no doubt.

"She'd always wanted kids." Sophie tipped her head down. "Guess she never got the chance."

The waitress shook her head. "In the end they said it was smoking that started the fire." The woman shifted her stance, beginning to move away. "Wanted a big wedding." She made a tsk-tsking noise with her mouth. "Crying shame."

Sophie's heart began a steady tapping in her chest. "Do you remember the fiancé's name?" She worked to keep her expression calm, her gut telling her this could be the big break in their investigation.

If they could track down the fiancé, maybe—just maybe—they'd be able to tie Cartwright to the Alexanders…and to Ally.

The woman looked down at the well-worn linoleum floor as though the town's history might be engraved in the tiles. She sucked in a sharp breath and pointed a finger at Sophie.

"Johnson. Kirk Johnson." A wide smile spread across her face. "I always knew those crossword puzzles would keep my mind sharp." She gestured to Sophie's cup. "Refill, hon?"

All Sophie could manage in response was a shake of her head. She sat in stunned silence, watching as the waitress moved on to the next table.

Kirk Johnson.

The man her sister had once loved, until he'd gotten violent…and threatening.

Kirk Johnson.

The man who had vanished after Rebecca had taken out a restraining order.

Kirk Johnson.

Robin's father.

Could Teresa Cartwright's Kirk Johnson be one and the same?

Sophie plucked her cell phone from her bag and punched in Gary's number. As the phone started ringing, she swallowed to clear the lump from her throat. When Gary answered, she opened her mouth to speak, but nothing came out.

"Soph? You all right?" The worry in Gary's voice was palpable across the line.

"Kirk Johnson." Sophie forced the words through the tightness squeezing at her throat.

"Who?" Gary's tone tightened.

"Robin's father." She dropped her voice to a whisper, not wanting to be overheard in the small restaurant.

"I'm not following you."

"Teresa Cartwright was engaged at the time of her death."

"To?"

"Kirk Johnson." A shudder slid through Sophie as she spoke the name. Another ghost from her past.

"Damn," Gary muttered. "We've got some work to do."

Sophie tossed a few bills on the table and climbed to her feet. "I'm on my way back."

As she made her way through the town back toward the hotel, she felt as though she were moving in slow motion while the world around her moved at a normal pace.

If Kirk Johnson had been involved with

Teresa Cartwright, it made sense he'd been involved in Becca's death as well as Teresa Cartwright's. And it made sense that Ally Alexander was one and the same as Robin Markham.

If the monster had murdered Becca and kidnapped Robin, Sophie would make him pay.

She squeezed her eyes shut momentarily and said a silent prayer to her sister.

She'd make him pay if it was the last thing she ever did.

Chapter Nine

When Sophie came through the door of Gary's hotel room, the mix of emotions plastered across her face shook him to the core. He'd grown accustomed to the polished, self-assured television personality facade, but this…this was real.

Perhaps searching for the truth behind her sister's death had begun to buff away at those sharp edges after all. And maybe his helping her had played some small part. Perhaps he'd begun to get under her skin as much as she'd gotten under his.

"You okay?" Gary wanted to say more, wanted to do more, but he held back, knowing better.

Pushing Sophie would only snap her emotional walls back into place—the walls that had disappeared at some point during the past few days. Moisture glistened in Sophie's eyes, and it took every ounce of willpower not to pull her into his arms.

"How could I not have dug deeper into Becca's death?" Sophie laughed, the sound a quick burst of frustration. "It's what I do, but I accepted what they told me. Why?"

The few remaining traces of her controlled facade crumbled and tears flooded her eyes. For once, she made no move to hide them.

"I heard you drove the authorities nuts with your questions."

A dark eyebrow arched and a look of something close to disbelief crossed Sophie's features. "You kept tabs on me?"

Gary opened his mouth to deny her accusation but decided to go for the truth instead.

"I did. What of it?" He shrugged. "I wondered how you were, that's all. Don't read anything more into it. You'd be wasting your time."

Her disbelief morphed into a visible sadness and she pressed her lips together, giving him a slow nod. "Me, too."

Now it was Gary's turn to narrow his eyes. "You, too, what?"

"I kept tabs on you." She blinked, shifting her gaze to the floor before giving Gary a look so vulnerable she could have knocked him over with a feather.

"I thought you didn't want any part of me in your life."

"I didn't." She tensed defensively. "I don't."

Sophie's words stung far worse than Gary would have imagined.

"I was curious." She gave a slight lift and drop of her shoulders. "Nothing more."

"Curious." He laughed. "I guess coming from someone as emotionally closed off as you are, that's a compliment."

Sophie's control cracked and her tears tumbled down her cheeks.

Regret surged through Gary. His comment had been cold and heartless. He was furious with her for threatening his family's sanctity *and* he still carried the hurt of their breakup, even though he'd tried to deny caring after all these years.

Suddenly, comforting Sophie became more important than proving her wrong.

Gary bundled her into his arms, holding tight, letting her sob until her shoulders finished shaking and her chest stopped heaving against his.

Her body relaxed beneath his touch, as if she'd never belonged anywhere else but in his arms. He winced. He needed to keep it together, now more than ever.

"I'm sorry," he whispered against her short, downy-soft hair.

Sophie shook her head. "I deserved that."

Her warm breath brushed against his neck and Gary's gut caught and twisted. Desire built inside him, edging its way through his system. He swallowed, working to keep hold of his control.

"I've tried so hard to keep everyone out." Her words continued—soft, flat, defeated. "But it didn't work."

Gary pushed her out to arm's length and smiled gently. Sophie reached to brush the moisture from her mascara-stained face. Bright pink splotches tinged her cheeks and the tip of her nose had gone red.

He'd never seen her look more beautiful.

She looked up at him through lashes glistening with tears. "Life finds you even when you shut it away."

Tell him about it. He'd vowed for years to keep Sophie out of his life, yet here she stood, safely cocooned inside his embrace. And as much as he'd always told himself rekindling any sort of attraction for Sophie would be wrong, at this particular moment, all Gary felt was right.

Sophie's throat worked. She looked so upset, so scared, that Gary could only think of one thing to do. He pressed a kiss to one cheek and then the other. When Sophie looked up at him again, something much more vibrant than sadness glimmered in her eyes. There, deep inside, was the spark of the girl he'd always known she kept hidden away.

Gary lowered his mouth to hers, tentatively at first, then more boldly, meeting Sophie move for move as she kissed him back, her lips parting, her tongue tangling with his.

Sophie didn't pull away, but rather wrapped her arms around his neck, tunneling her fingers into his hair. Hot, pent-up desire threatened to explode inside Gary.

He shifted her closer, pulling the length of

her body against his, shuddering at the feel of her soft curves pressed to his firm chest, the feel of his hard length against her stomach.

"I was wrong," Sophie murmured against his mouth and Gary was lost. "If you shut everyone out, you end up with nothing."

He hoisted her in one smooth move, never breaking their kiss, anchoring her in his arms, one arm beneath her, the other pulling her tighter still to him.

Gary lowered her gently to the bed, then released her, sitting beside her, the cheap hotel mattress sagging beneath their weight. Sophie swallowed again, and he narrowed his eyes.

Was this a huge mistake? Had she meant what she'd said? Or was she acting out in a moment of grief and heartache? Worse, was she encouraging his sexual advance to weaken his defenses when it came to Maggie and Ally?

"Sophie, I—"

She shook her head, life glittering in her dark brown eyes. "No more talking." She pressed a finger to his lips.

All of Gary's questions and doubts vanished, his brain and body focused on one thing.

Sophie.

He planned to comfort her, caress her, make love to her until she fell asleep—safe in his embrace.

He kissed her fully then, trailing his lips down the line of her jaw to her neck when she arched her back in response to his touch.

Gary's pulse roared in his ears, memories of the passion they'd once shared battling with the reality that they were now on opposite sides of the issue of Ally's true identity. When Sophie emitted a soft moan from somewhere deep inside her throat, all thoughts of Ally and Maggie and Kirk Johnson fled his mind.

He pulled Sophie to him, enfolding her in his arms, surrounding her with comfort. With security. With protection. No matter what else might happen over the course of the investigation, one thing was certain. He'd keep Sophie safe, no matter what she believed about his niece.

No matter what she'd done or said in the past, the bold-faced truth was that his heart still belonged to the woman in his arms. He'd neither been able to move on nor move past her memory since that night seven years earlier when she'd walked out of his life.

He retraced a path along her neck, back to her lips. As Sophie's lips parted to welcome him—tasting, teasing—she murmured his name.

The sound of his name on her lips detonated hot desire deep inside him.

He lowered her gently, leaning to one side to trace the front placket of her suit, parting the fabric button by button.

When her lacy bra peeked from beneath the conservative weave of her suit, Gary's stomach caught and twisted.

Sophie's eyes locked with his and they held their stare for a moment, the silence between them speaking volumes about the attraction and chemistry that remained even after all of the precious time they'd lost.

"Are you sure?" He spoke softly, drawing a finger along the line of her jaw.

Sophie's only response was the hint of a smile at the corner of her luscious lips and the slightest nod of her head.

Gary freed the front clasp of her bra, exposing the creamy flesh. He cupped one breast, stroking her nipple until it beaded beneath his touch. He dragged the back of his fingers along the valley between her breasts, turning his hand to caress and cup, explore and massage.

Sophie moaned and arched her back, pressing her body into his touch. Gary's own body screamed with an urgent need he'd never known, not even with Sophie years before. He lowered his mouth, taking one pert nipple lightly between his teeth, suckling the soft flesh and teasing her with his tongue. She writhed beneath him, her fingers winding their way into his hair, urging him on.

Abandon and desire tangled inside him, and he found Sophie's sudden lack of inhibition more heady than any fantasies he'd harbored for her over the years.

He trailed his hand down the curve of her waist to the soft flesh of her hip, sliding his grip to cup her rear end, pulling her toward him. He shifted positions, dropping his mouth lower and lower still until he hit the waistband of her skirt.

Excitement pulsed through him when Sophie reached to free the clasp of her skirt then wriggled the soft material down over her legs, exposing lacy panties that matched her bra and the sexiest pair of thigh-high stockings he'd ever seen.

For all of her careful containment when it came to her heart and outer appearance, the sight of Sophie, flushed with desire, wearing nothing but lacy underwear and stockings spoke volumes about the passionate woman trapped inside. The passionate woman he'd once tried to set free and had every intention of setting free now.

Sophie caught him studying her and a sudden hint of embarrassment lit in her eyes. Before she could speak, or have second thoughts, Gary pressed his mouth to the hot fabric between her legs. He flicked his tongue through the lace, tasting her sweetness, driving his pulse to a frenzied pitch. He cupped her buttocks fully now, pressing her tightly to his mouth, tracing his tongue along the edge of the flimsy fabric, teasing his way to her bare flesh.

He deftly pushed the scrap of lace out of his way, finding her wet and waiting. Sophie's sharp intake of breath told him she'd surrendered to the undeniable heat sparking between them.

When she wriggled out of her panties, Gary longed to strip out of his jeans and drive inside of her, deep and hard, but he held back. He mustered every ounce of control to pleasure her first, to prove he wanted more than to satisfy his own sexual tension—he wanted to coax her to emotional and physical abandon.

He flicked his tongue against her tender flesh, then drank deeply, urging her toward her release. He shifted one hand to her waist, then higher, cupping her breast and finding her nipple, teasing the firm peak between his thumb and forefinger. When Sophie's breathing quickened and she murmured his name, he didn't slow, but rather quickened his motions, pushing her, challenging her, urging her to let go.

When her sharp breathing gave way to a series of moans, he pulled away, moving quickly to undress, sheath himself with protection and lower himself between her legs.

Sophie opened to him fully, wrapping her knees around his waist as he eased inside her.

"You okay?" The tight emotion in his voice surprised him, but Sophie's response eased his lingering doubt.

"I've always been ready for you." Their gazes locked, and Gary rocked inside her, slowly at first, then more quickly. Harder and deeper, his eyes never leaving hers, her eyes never leaving his.

When she gasped and her body began to pulse around him, he thrust and held, holding her close as the waves of her release crashed over her.

The flush of sexual release on her face was more than his control could handle and he gave up the battle to control his body, surrendering to his own orgasm, sinking into her, savoring every moment, every sensation of their joining.

SOPHIE STRUGGLED TO HOLD on to some scrap of control as the rhythm of Gary's lovemaking drove her over the edge.

Her breath caught and the room spun as one orgasm followed another.

Gary dropped a kiss to her mouth, finding her tongue with his as he slowed the movement of their bodies, holding her close. He kissed her with abandon, then pushed himself above her again, driving her yet again to the edge.

She breathed in sharply, working to calm the frantic beating of her heart.

"Stop thinking," he whispered. "Just feel."

Then he gripped her buttocks and drove himself fully inside her, smiling as she surrendered once again to the ecstasy of release.

A long while later, she woke, still wrapped in his embrace. She snuggled against him, safe in his arms, protected, loved.

Then reality came crashing down over her like a cold shower.

She was no better than her mother, seeking solace in the arms of a man. She'd no sooner received the news about Kirk Johnson than she'd run to Gary, throwing herself at him like a spineless female who needed sex to soothe her wounded soul.

Sophie wriggled free of his embrace and sat up on the edge of the bed.

Tears stung at her eyes. She'd slipped. She'd given in to the attraction she still felt for the man. What a mistake.

She stood and moved quietly toward the bathroom, plucking her overnight bag from the chair where Gary had dropped it. To think, he'd put her bag in his room until she could get checked in, and instead of her doing so, she'd made love to him, spending the night in his bed.

Sophie pulled the bathroom door closed behind her, dropped her bag and cranked on the shower faucet, feeling no better than a two-bit hooker.

If she planned to track down Kirk Johnson and prove Ally was her biological niece, she'd better do a much better job at ignoring the impact Gary had on her heart.

GARY'S CELL PHONE RANG just as he was staring at Sophie's empty pillow. A hint of dawn eased around the heavy curtains, and regret whispered at the base of his brain.

He knew Sophie, and if she'd sneaked out of bed and into the shower this early in the morning, her conscience and self-control had kicked in big time.

He snapped to attention when he heard Randy Simpson's voice on the line.

"The man's a ghost."

"Johnson?" The rush of adrenaline tingled in Gary's veins.

"Vanished into thin air."

"Damn it."

Silence beat between them and Gary could imagine the smug grin on his friend's face. He knew him too well.

"What?" he asked. "You found something. If you didn't, you'd be tossing out theories left and right."

Simpson's chuckle sounded low across the line. "It's more of what I didn't find."

Gary scrubbed a hand across his face in frustration, all the while eyeing the bathroom door and doing his best to ignore the sound of the shower.

"Not following you."

"What I didn't find—" Simpson continued "—was any trace of Johnson from the day Cartwright died forward."

"How is that possible?" Gary frowned.

"The man disappeared."

"But how?"

Simpson made a snapping noise with his mouth. "Maybe he came into a lot of cash."

"Anything new on Cartwright?"

"Nothing," Simpson answered. "No leftover bank accounts. No record of live births."

Gary pressed his eyes shut. Damn. A

definite theory had taken root in his brain. If Kirk Johnson and Cartwright had been involved, there was a distinct possibility the two had been in on the adoption together. If Cartwright had never given birth, the child she placed for adoption may very well have been Becca Markham's infant daughter.

Johnson could have instructed Cartwright to turn over the infant in exchange for cash. Then he'd eliminated the only risk to exposure—Cartwright—and he'd taken her money and run, literally.

"Think he left the country?"

"Can't find a thing to confirm that," Simpson answered. "It's more like he ceased to exist."

Gary sat deep in thought after they broke off the call. If he weren't Ally's uncle, he'd have no problem jumping to the obvious conclusion.

The child had been taken out of her home before the fire and passed off as Cartwright's. Then she'd been adopted by a couple desperate for a child. A couple who didn't ask questions and who didn't want to know anything more than they needed to know—that they loved their new daughter.

His heart twisted in his chest.

He and Sophie had yet to uncover any hard evidence, but the puzzle pieces were certainly falling into place.

What if Sophie had been right from the beginning?

Gary had been wrong to think his niece couldn't possibly be her niece, but he had been right about one thing.

He'd do whatever it took to protect his sister and her family. Regardless of whether or not Ally was actually Robin Markham, Maggie and Robert were the only parents she'd ever known.

Removing the child from their home could only lead to heartache and emotional turmoil.

No matter how he felt about Sophie, he couldn't let her win. He had to put his own family first.

And he would.

He'd no sooner resigned himself to his decision than his cell rang again.

SOPHIE TURNED IN THE DIRECTION of the bathroom door, letting the shower's spray cascade down her side. She could have sworn she heard something, felt someone watching her.

Gary. She'd not only become careless, she was fast becoming paranoid.

She drew in a deep breath and released it as an exasperated sigh.

What a fool she was to have let him see her weakness last night. Hell, to have let him see…everything.

She couldn't remember the last time she'd allowed herself to feel anything so completely as she had let herself feel every moment of their lovemaking.

Gary had matured into a man who knew how to comfort and please a woman—to comfort and please her. But she wasn't looking for comfort and pleasure, and she had no right to let him think any differently.

She'd broken her promise never to fall for a man when she'd fallen for Gary during college, and she'd responded by doing the only thing she knew how to do.

She'd walked away.

As before, there was only one thing to do now. Walk away again. And she would.

Just as soon as they'd finished their investigation and she'd reclaimed Ally as the niece she'd once known and loved.

Sophie twisted off the shower faucet and reached for a towel, drying herself off quickly. She rubbed the moisture out of her hair, fluffed the short strands with her fingers, and checked her reflection in the mirror.

Her complexion glowed and her eyes held a light she hadn't seen there in a very long time. Hell, she'd never seen herself look so alive.

She'd just discovered her sister had more than likely been murdered, and here Sophie stood looking like the cat who'd eaten the canary.

All the more reason to make a clean break with Gary now, before anything more than one night of lovemaking developed.

The man was a distraction. A distraction she couldn't afford, and a distraction she didn't want.

Sophie eyed the burgundy suit she'd packed in her bag, but reached for a faded pair of blue jeans instead. She shimmied into the worn denim, sighing at the brush of the smooth fabric against her skin.

The jeans zipped easily—perhaps too

easily. It had been months since she'd worn them and she'd obviously dropped weight. Too many long hours at work, no doubt, but that was the way success was achieved in her business.

She pulled a buttery yellow sweater over her head, gathered her personal items and stepped out into the bedroom.

Gary sat on the bed, dressed, his bag packed beside him. Maybe dealing with what had transpired between them would be easier than she'd thought. It looked as though regret had firmly entrenched itself into his thoughts, as well.

"It was a mistake, wasn't it?" she asked.

He turned to face her, a frown creasing the skin between his eyes, his expression a mix of surprise and disbelief. He thinned his lips, then laughed softly, knowingly.

"Is that what took you so long in there?" He tipped his head toward the bathroom. "Trying to wash off every trace of last night?"

Before Sophie could answer, Gary sprang to his feet, hoisting his bag over his shoulder.

Tact had never been one of her strong suits, and apparently she'd blown it once again in that department.

"Gary, I—"

"It was a mistake, Soph," he said as he stepped out into the cool morning. He turned back to face her, his features set and determined, yet unreadable. "Maggie called. Robert's regained consciousness. We need to go."

Excitement kicked to life in Sophie's veins, easing out the anxiety she'd felt over the awkwardness dancing in the air between them. She slipped into her shoes, grabbed her purse and bag and followed him.

As she dropped into the passenger seat and slammed the door closed, she reached for his arm, surprise splashing through her when he pulled away from her touch.

"Last night never happened, Soph." Gary cranked the ignition, backing the car out of the parking spot in one fluid motion. "It was nothing more than a way to find comfort in the midst of the craziness. You know it. I know it. Let it go."

She opened her mouth to answer, but he continued before she could utter a word.

"I decided to make that move to Los Angeles. I'll be gone before the month's out.

By that time, you'll have found out exactly what happened to your sister and niece, and if, in fact, my niece is your niece, chances are you and I will never speak kindly to each other again."

He pulled the car to a stop where the side road met the highway and pinned Sophie with a glare. Anger danced in his steely look.

"I'll never forgive you if you break my sister's heart. Understood? One of us is not going to get the answer we want at the end of this investigation. And if that person is me, I'm going to fight you tooth and nail for that little girl's right to stay with the only parents she's ever known."

Even though Gary's words stung, Sophie knew he was absolutely correct. There never had been a future for the two of them. And there never would be.

The only thing that mattered now was making the connection between Robin and Ally's adoption.

Once that piece of the puzzle was put into play, Gary would have to admit she was right.

And if she broke his sister's heart in the meantime, so be it. Robin belonged with her only living relative. For that, Sophie would give up just about anything, including her precious career and long hours.

Uncertainty whispered at the base of her brain. Could she do it? Could she raise a child? Lord knew she'd never been close to anyone except Becca. She'd never let herself make a commitment of the heart to anyone.

That's when she realized she only needed to remember one thing. The child was the precious daughter of her beloved sister. Surely her heart would open up to let Robin in.

A calm assurance spread through her.

Matter of fact, she'd already let the little girl into her heart, and she'd do anything to prove she was her niece and get her back. Hell, she'd just about sign over her soul.

If that wasn't commitment, Sophie didn't know what was.

There was one thing she wouldn't do. She would never back down from the fight out of friendship or attraction to Gary.

Robin's welfare was the only thing that mattered, and Sophie vowed to do whatever it took to ensure the child ended up where she rightfully belonged.

She'd never before let her heart rule her head, even though she'd come close—with Gary.

Sophie hadn't given in then, and she wasn't about to give in now.

And if he thought any differently, he had another think coming.

Chapter Ten

They rode in silence during the rest of the drive back to Philadelphia. With every mile that registered on the odometer, Gary mentally berated himself for being such an idiot.

He'd let Sophie under his skin.

He should have known better. Much better.

Sophie Markham was everything he loathed about women *and* the world of television news. She'd become a walking, talking plastic monument to viewer ratings and focus-group feedback. Even worse, she'd used her career as an excuse to increase her avoidance of emotional entanglements.

Not that what they'd shared had been an entanglement. Apparently what they'd shared was better termed a convenient night of lovemaking at a low point in Sophie's life.

So be it.

He turned his Mustang into an open spot near the hospital's visitor entrance, cut the ignition and climbed out before Sophie had the time to unhook her seat belt.

He set out at a clip, not caring whether she followed him or not.

The most frustrating part of his entire day had been the moment she'd emerged from the bathroom. When she'd spoken, he'd been momentarily stunned by her appearance.

Tousled hair. Blue jeans. A casual sweater.

At that moment, he realized she was the most beautiful woman he'd ever seen. He'd also let his guard down for the briefest moment, thinking the night before had gotten through to her cold heart.

How wrong he'd been.

He stopped at the nurses' station at the entrance to the wing where Robert was recovering.

"Robert Alexander?"

He caught Sophie's pissed-off expression out of the corner of his eye just as the nurse rattled off the room number.

"Thanks," he said, making a beeline for the room.

When he cleared the doorway, he spotted Maggie, head close to her husband's, talking softly as Robert slept.

"Hey." Gary dropped his voice to a whisper as he entered the room.

Gratitude shone in Maggie's eyes as he neared. "You're here. He was so frantic."

Gary frowned, hesitating when he heard the click of Sophie's shoes as she followed him into the room.

He tipped his head toward Robert and narrowed his gaze on his sister's worried features. "What's up?"

"I told him about Brian Franklin's accident and he didn't buy it."

"The accident?"

Sophie's voice sounded close to Gary's ear. He stepped toward his sister, squatting down to drop a kiss to her cheek and to press a hand to Robert's arm.

Maggie glanced from Gary to Sophie, then back again.

Gary nodded. "It's okay."

Maggie drew in a slow breath, and if Gary

wasn't mistaken, the color drained from her cheeks. "He remembers who referred Teresa Cartwright to them. It was a former client of Franklin's."

Gary's pulse quickened. A former client? That could explain Franklin's "accident." If whoever made the original referral had somehow kidnapped the Markham infant and passed her off as his own, or as Cartwright's, chances were he'd come looking for anyone who posed a possibility of exposure.

The fact Robert had been beaten half to death, and Franklin was dead, gave credibility to the theory.

"Bad news."

The sound of his brother-in-law's voice snapped Gary's focus to the bed. Robert worked to hold his eyes open, his mouth set in a grim line.

"Who?" Gary asked. "Teresa Cartwright?"

Robert gave a slight shake of his head, wincing at the small movement. "Guy who sent her. Brian had represented him as a juvenile. The guy knew Brian could keep a secret. Figured he could make the placement."

"And you stepped in to offer the home."

The tone of Sophie's voice filled Gary with anger. Now wasn't the time to pull any holier-than-thou act she might have been holding back.

He shot her a warning glare and she fell silent.

Robert nodded, looking ashamed. "I did. I won't lie. I wanted to give my wife a family."

"Did the woman have proof she was the birth mother?"

"No."

"So Ally could have been someone else's biological daughter?"

Silence hung in the room, the icy tension broken only by the tick of the hospital clock hanging on the far wall.

Robert looked only at Maggie as he answered. "Yes."

Tears glistened in Maggie's eyes and Gary's heart hurt. Robert had done what any grieving father and husband might have done, given the chance. He'd seized an opportunity to help heal his family's emotional wounds. Right or wrong, he'd done what he'd thought he had to do.

His sister would never survive losing Ally. Never.

Gary shook off the thought and focused. The only thing he could do now was to keep working through the puzzle of clues. He gathered his thoughts, working to keep his emotion out of his voice. "Do you remember a name?"

Robert nodded. "Need to warn you first."

Gary frowned. "Why?"

Robert shuddered and Maggie pressed a hand to his cheek. "Maybe this is all too much for you right now."

Her husband cut his eyes at her. "This guy was dangerous. Brian used to say he was the only client who had ever scared him. Something about his eyes."

"What did he defend him for?"

Robert hesitated. "It's a sealed record."

Gary swore inwardly. Juvenile cases usually were. But he didn't need to worry whether or not Robert would talk. His mouth was already moving.

"He torched his grandparents' house—" Robert paused before he finished his sentence "—with them inside."

Sophie and Maggie uttered a collective gasp. Gary scowled. The guy had killed his grandparents?

"On purpose?" he asked.

Robert nodded. "Did his time in a juvenile facility. Referred Cartwright to Franklin years later."

"What's his name, Robert?"

Robert's gaze narrowed and Gary held his breath. They needed this piece of information to break the case wide open. Gary stole a glance at Sophie's face, noting the wide-eyed expectancy he saw there.

"Go on," Maggie said, giving her husband's hand a pat. "If this guy attacked you, I want him found before he can hurt you or... anyone else...again."

Or Ally, Gary thought. The unspoken fear glistened in his sister's eyes.

Robert frowned, but pressed through his obvious hesitancy. "Kirk Johnson."

Gary's gut clenched and, based on the expression on Sophie's face, hers had done the same.

"Oh my God." Sophie paled.

Robert looked from Sophie to Gary. Gary shot him a quick frown. "You're sure?"

Robert nodded. "Brian always said it was the damnedest thing. The kid's expression never changed." He rubbed a hand across his mouth. "Said there was no description that did the look justice."

"Without a soul." Sophie spoke in such a low tone Robert frowned, apparently having missed what she'd said.

When Sophie met his gaze, Gary twisted up his features, letting her know they hadn't understood her.

She straightened, pulling herself into her confident, camera-worthy stance even though she stood in the middle of a hospital room looking nothing like a top television reporter.

Sophie leaned closer, wincing before she spoke the words. "Kirk Johnson always looked as though he had no soul."

The light of recognition spread across Robert's face. He nodded. "That's exactly what Brian said."

"Did you know him?" Maggie asked, looking directly at Sophie.

Sophie nodded, moisture shining in her

own eyes. "He killed my sister—" she hesitated, her throat working "—in a house fire."

Angry as he was with her, Gary felt sympathy for Sophie. He knew she was right. Every investigative bone in his body told him Kirk Johnson had set the fire that had killed Becca Markham. Just as he'd murdered Teresa Cartwright.

It made sense that he'd killed Cartwright to eliminate a witness to the illegal adoption, but why had he killed Becca?

But that question wasn't the only one looming large in Gary's mind.

No. His thoughts centered elsewhere—on the question that had brought them all to this point in the first place.

Did Robin Markham perish along with her mother in the fire? Or had she somehow been removed from the home? And if so, where was she?

An image of the identical butterfly birthmarks flashed through Gary's mind's eye, and his heart hit the pit of his stomach.

His gut told him Robin and Ally were one and the same child, even though his heart wasn't ready to accept that truth.

"Was the paperwork legal?" Sophie's tone wavered, full of emotion.

Robert grimaced, taking his time before he answered. Gary had known his brother-in-law long enough to know what the pause meant. The attorney was searching for the right word, the most appropriate turn of phrase.

Gary knew Robert's answer before he spoke.

"No." Robert's eyes never wavered from Sophie's.

Maggie burst into tears and moved away from the bed, crossing to the window where she stared out at the late afternoon sun bouncing off the Philadelphia skyline.

"It was legal in that Cartwright signed the surrender," Robert continued.

"With no proof she was the birth mother?" Moisture glistened in Sophie's eyes.

"No." Robert thinned his lips. "And we didn't wait the six months required before we finalized the placement."

"You and Franklin pushed through everything yourselves?" Sophie continued. "No state involvement? No agency involvement? No one else knew?"

"No one." Robert pulled himself up taller

in the bed, and Gary realized his brother-in-law wasn't sorry for the choice he'd made.

"Who do you think came after you, Robert?"

Sophie had moved closer, hanging on his every word.

Robert shook his head. "I didn't see him." A bitter chuckle slipped from his lips. "I was trying to find the file for you two, and it took my brain too long to realize someone had entered my office."

"How do you know that?" Sophie's voice climbed a few octaves, hope blatant in her tone.

Robert closed his eyes and shook his head ever so slightly. "One minute I was staring at spots of paint on a pair of boots and the next I was waking up here this morning."

Gary swallowed, not wanting to jump to the obvious conclusion. "Spots of paint?"

Robert blinked. "Looked like a face. Isn't that ridiculous?"

But Gary knew it wasn't ridiculous at all. Whoever had attacked John Cook and Sophie had attacked Robert. And the suspect was obvious.

Kirk Johnson.

A man who had a past to protect, at least

two apparent murders to cover up and a kidnapping to explain.

He turned to Sophie, but she was already moving toward the door. When their eyes met, that morning's argument seemed inconsequential.

Their differences could wait until later.

For now, they needed to focus on one thing, and one thing only.

Finding Kirk Johnson before he could harm anyone else.

Chapter Eleven

"You can't stay here alone," Gary said as he pulled into Sophie's driveway.

"I most certainly can."

They'd spent the evening searching for Kirk Johnson through every resource the *Inquirer* offices had to offer. They'd found a steady paper trail of addresses, including the address Johnson had briefly shared with Sophie's sister.

There was only one problem. The man's trail ended cold the day after Teresa Cartwright had died, just as Simpson had said.

After the emotions of the day and the frustrating search, not to mention the seven-hour return drive from Bradston, Sophie wanted nothing more than to crawl into bed.

Her head hurt, her stomach was empty and

her heart ached. She'd failed to save her sister from Johnson, a man she'd disliked from the moment she'd first set eyes on him. Her words of warning hadn't been enough. The restraining order hadn't been enough. And, after her sister's death, apparently her investigation hadn't been enough.

Regret flooded her heart. She was a top reporter, for God's sake. How could she not have pushed harder, dug deeper, when it had been her own sister's death she'd been questioning?

She'd failed.

She'd failed Becca and she'd failed Robin.

Now, Sophie would give anything to know what had happened—to know what had driven Johnson to murder. Had it been solely to kidnap his daughter, Robin? But why?

According to Becca, Johnson had never had anything but contempt for the child. Robin had been the reason Becca had finally put her foot down against his abuse. She'd wanted him as far away from their child as possible.

His kidnapping Robin in a grasp at custody made no sense. But his kidnapping Robin in a grasp for a hefty adoption fee made all the sense in the world.

It fit his personality to a tee.

Sophie sank back against the passenger seat and let her weary eyes close. When Gary spoke, his voice jolted her, and she sat bolt upright in the seat, doing her best not to look taken aback.

She turned to face him, only to be greeted by raised brows.

"Deep thoughts?"

Sophie shot him a glare then pushed open the passenger door, reaching into the back seat for her overnight bag.

Gary grasped her hand and held tight. Surprise skittered through her at the way her stomach clenched at the feel of his skin against hers.

"What are you doing?" She felt the heat of her indignation rising in her cheeks.

"You are not staying here alone." His expression was grim, the set of his jaw firm, determined. He drew out the sentence, punctuating each word as if it were a separate message.

Sophie narrowed her gaze. "Let go of my hand."

Pinpricks of sensation scorched outward from his touch, much to her dismay. Her head might be regretting their night together, but her body apparently felt anything but.

"I'll sleep on your sofa." Gary released his grip and reached for his own overnight bag. "Trust me, I won't be making any attempts to share your bed."

"Fine."

Sophie did her best to ignore the sensation of his stare on her backside as she closed the distance between the car and her front door. After she'd stepped inside and dropped her bag in the foyer, Gary did the same, only he kept walking. Straight for the kitchen.

"Where are you going?" She frowned, wanting nothing more than for him to turn around and leave.

"Kitchen," he called out over his shoulder. "I'm starving."

"Make yourself at home," she grumbled.

"Thanks, I will."

Sophie cringed as she heard the refrigerator door ease open. As much as she hated to admit it, she was famished and wouldn't mind one of whatever Gary was about to serve up.

"Still like cheese in your omelet?" he called out.

Sophie licked her lips in response. "Sure." She did her best to sound nonchalant. There was no way in hell she'd let Gary know she was actually relieved to have him here, let alone cooking for her.

The thought of Kirk Johnson anywhere in the vicinity of Philadelphia and South Jersey sent cold chills down her spine.

Robert's ex-partner had been right.

Kirk Johnson had dead eyes as well as a dead heart.

The last thing she wanted was to be the object of his hatred, though, based on both Cook's and Robert's descriptions of their attacker's boots, she'd probably already received her warning. Though she hadn't listened.

She closed her eyes and tried to remember the man's voice. The man's touch.

Next time, you won't live to talk about it.

Her stomach lurched and she leaned against the wall for support. Dread swirled inside her, knotting into a ball of fear she couldn't deny.

The man was capable of anything, and they had to stop him. They also had to get him to admit to Robin's kidnapping and adoptive placement.

"Hey."

Sophie blinked her eyes open at the feel of Gary's hand against her cheek.

"You okay?" he asked. "I called you twice but you were totally zoned out. Where'd you go?"

"The past." She offered a weak smile as she pushed away from the wall and headed for the kitchen.

"Good past?" Gary asked as he trailed behind her. "Or bad past."

"Bad." Sophie salivated at the sight of the dishes Gary had prepared, but the thought of Kirk Johnson turned her stomach and she had to swallow down her gag. "Very bad."

GARY WOKE FROM HIS DREAM with a start. His head had slid sideways along the arm of the sofa and his neck had grown stiff and painful in its awkward position.

A foreign noise teased at the edge of his consciousness and he pushed through the fog of his fatigue, battling to bring himself fully awake.

An acrid smell filled his senses and he

snapped awake instantly, launching himself to his feet even as he struggled to blink the sleep from his eyes.

How long had he been out? He eyed the mug of coffee on the end table next to where he'd slept. Full. Untouched.

So much for his future as a bodyguard.

Something crackled and he spun, slowly, trepidation seeping through his every pore. Something was wrong. Very wrong.

The glow of licking, surging flames filled the center hall. Gary struggled for focus, struggled to wrap his brain around the sight before him. This wasn't a dream. This was the real thing.

Fire.

He had to wake Sophie before the flames reached the second floor.

"Sophie!"

He screamed her name as he yanked open the pantry in the hall, scanning the floor inside for any sign of a fire extinguisher.

Empty.

His pulse pounded in his ears, almost, but not quite, drowning out the sound of the hissing flames.

Adrenaline pumped in his veins.

Something crashed behind him and he spotted movement in the mudroom. A solitary figure, all in black, moving with skill and ease toward the back door.

Johnson?

The flames grew hotter beside Gary and he had to choose. Pursue the intruder or save Sophie.

The choice was a no-brainer.

If anything happened to her, he'd never forgive himself. And as loath as he was to admit it, he cared for her, cared what happened to her.

Fate might have conspired to keep them apart and put them at odds, but Gary couldn't imagine a world without Sophie in it.

He grabbed the blanket from the sofa and drenched it in the kitchen sink. Wrapping it around himself as he ran, he hurtled headlong through the growing smoke and flames. He hit the stairs in an all-out sprint, taking them two at a time, all the while screaming Sophie's name.

Her bedroom door sat closed when he reached it, and fear gripped his throat and squeezed.

She had to be alive. This time, Johnson's plan had to fail. It had to.

"Sophie!"

"Something's wrong," she screamed in answer. "I can't get out."

Without looking for a lock or a jamb, Gary hit the door with every ounce of force he could muster, slamming his full body weight, shoulder-first into the heavy wood.

Something cracked, and he tried again, doing his best to ignore the pain slicing through his body. This time, the door gave way and he catapulted into the room.

Sophie stood wide-eyed, her face full of shock and fear.

A swirl of smoke hovered at ceiling height and Gary gripped her by the elbows, studying her wide, scared eyes. "You okay?"

She nodded. "How are we going to get out of here?"

Gary turned her toward the window, knowing the stairs were too dangerous to try again. Sirens sounded in the distance, growing nearer.

"I hit 911 as soon as I realized what was happening."

No one could ever say the woman wasn't sharp. "Good thinking." He urged her forward. "Let's move."

The window opened easily and Gary twisted it inward, removing it from its frame and tossing it aside.

He glanced outside. They were in luck. The flames hadn't spread to the area below the bedroom and the angled garage roof was well within their reach as long as they were careful.

Flashing lights sliced through the night sky as he hoisted Sophie through the window, keeping a death grip on her hand until she'd safely negotiated her footing and had moved onto the lower roof.

He followed quickly behind her, looping one arm around her waist to support her. Glass shattered behind them—another bedroom window. They'd gotten out just in time.

Gary lowered himself to the edge of the roof, hanging to stretch as far as he could before he released his grip and dropped to the ground. Sophie followed and he gripped her by the waist, easing her fall.

They raced hand in hand away from the

house and out to the street just as the fire trucks arrived and their crews launched into action.

Gary took one look at the shocked expression on Sophie's face and pulled her into his arms. Much to his surprise, she didn't resist, but rather wrapped her arms around his waist and buried her face in his chest.

He dropped a kiss to the top of her head and held her tightly. Relief began to edge out the adrenaline in his veins, but he couldn't shake the image of what might have happened had Sophie been alone.

Johnson's latest fire might have claimed yet another life. He shuddered, pulling her more tightly to him, knowing she'd pull away before long, but savoring the feel of her relatively unharmed body against his in the meantime.

"It's going to be all right," he whispered against her hair, but as he looked at the raging fire and the flames now licking at the edge of the home's roof, he began to wonder if everything would ever be all right again.

SOPHIE STARED AT the burned-out shell of her home, waiting for her tears to start, but feeling nothing.

Shock. Gary kept telling her she was in shock, but she couldn't process that thought. Matter of fact, she couldn't process much of anything.

The paramedics had given her a blanket after they'd checked her out and declared her unharmed, save for a few scrapes and bruises from her narrow escape.

If Gary hadn't stayed the night, she might have… well…she might not have survived to solve the mystery of her sister's death.

Gary stood huddled with the fire investigator a few feet away, and Sophie moved closer, straining to hear their conversation.

"Whoever set the blaze wasn't worried about leaving a trail. Seems he was only worried about setting a fire hot enough to do the job quickly."

The fire investigator shook his head, letting a cynical burst of laughter slip between his lips. "Bastard knew what he was doing. The batteries had been taken from each detector. If you hadn't been there, she might not have made it out of that room."

Sophie shuddered, not for the first time.

Gary scowled. "But I was right there on the

sofa. If someone had taken the batteries from the smoke detectors, I'd have heard them."

The investigator gave a tight smile. "Not a pro. A pro would have removed them earlier on. He'd have left the smallest number of tasks for last minute." He patted Gary on the shoulder. "Signs of accelerant usage are blatant. He didn't even try to make it look like an accident. Probably got in, completed his setup, lit a few matches and got out."

Gary dropped his voice low. "Did the police tell you I saw him?"

The investigator nodded. "We've got the description."

Excitement kicked to life in Sophie's veins. Gary hadn't told her he'd seen anything.

"Not much of a description."

Gary was speaking again, even more softly. Sophie moved in tighter.

"I had to find Sophie. There wasn't time to chase him."

Gratitude surged through her. She truly did owe Gary her life.

"You'd be surprised what small detail might break the case wide open," the investigator said.

Gary turned, looking startled when he

spotted her standing so closely. "Don't you have an extinguisher?"

She nodded, pulling the heavy blanket more tightly around her shoulders. "In the pantry."

"Then he must have taken that, too." Gary turned back to the investigator. "It was missing."

The other man nodded. "Doesn't match any of our other cases, but you can be sure we'll check the database. I'll be in touch, Ms. Markham." He shot her a kind smile. "You have some place to go?"

Some place to go.

Sophie's heart fell to her toes.

No. She didn't have some place to go. Everything she'd owned had been inside her house, now a smoldering wreck.

"Sure." She forced the word through her disbelief. "I'll be fine."

But would she? She had nothing but the clothes on her back—a pair of battered flannel pajamas she'd had since college. Hell, even her feet were bare.

She'd lost everything. Clothes. Possessions. Reporting awards. Story notes. Her purse. Credit cards.

Her stomach pitched and rolled, bile choking her.

More important than everything else, she'd lost her most treasured possession—every last trace of Becca and Robin.

Where she'd once believed her career was everything, now she knew better. Mementos of her loved ones were the most important items she'd possessed.

And now they were gone forever.

She sensed Gary's stare and looked up into his worried eyes.

"Where will you go?" he asked.

Sophie shrugged. "There's a cot at the station. I could just go there for now."

"Media's going to have a field day with this once they get wind of it." Gary's worry lines deepened.

Damn. She sagged with fatigue. "I hadn't thought of that."

"Our plan to keep this quiet might be about to blow up in our faces."

Sophie said nothing, trying to think through what excuse she could give if questioned by fellow reporters. "What if I theorized this attack was an escalation of the attack at the station?"

Gary closed the space between them and dragged his knuckles across her cheek. Her stomach clenched. He gripped her shoulder and squeezed.

"You and I both know this is an escalation of that attack. And you're lucky you weren't killed. But, if the media thinks this is related to the other attacks on reporters, we could buy ourselves some time."

"And keep Ally out of the system." Sophie's heart ached. She'd do whatever it took to avoid that development. As long as Ally was with Maggie and Robert, she'd have a loving home. That much was certain.

"We need to tell Maggie what's happened." Gary tightened his grip on Sophie's shoulder. "And we need to get you settled somewhere other than at the station."

"I can go to a hotel. Maybe they'll trust me on the credit-card number. I know it by heart."

Gary lifted a brow. "You don't know anyone well enough to stay with them?"

"No." She shook her head, suddenly ashamed of her pathetic social life.

She had no one.

Her plan to remain emotionally unattached

had worked beautifully. She'd lived alone, existed alone, and now—in a time of need— she was wholly, fully, completely alone.

Sophie drew in a steadying breath. "Only Cook and his family, but I'm the last thing he needs."

"You'll stay with me then."

The certainty in Gary's eyes shook her to her core.

"That's not necessary, but thank you."

Her words belied the emotions battling inside her. She was wavering from her earlier words about their being together being a mistake. A very real part of her longed to stay with him tonight. Longed to know he was near and would keep her safe, when everything around her seemed to be shifting out of control.

Gary stepped close and dropped his gaze from her eyes to her mouth then back. "I won't take no for an answer."

"But I—"

He pressed a finger to her lips, cutting her off mid-sentence. His touch was brief but firm, his message clear.

"No buts. I won't let you be alone. Not now."

Sophie's pulse quickened, knowing what she had to say to him—what had to be spoken out loud. For the record.

"I've lost everything, Gary."

"I know. I'm sorry."

He turned, taking her arm to steer her toward his car. Sophie jerked free of his touch, and Gary spun around, brows furrowed.

"I need you to hear me on this," she said, heart tapping a rapid beat against her ribs. "I lost Robin once."

His eyes widened, his features falling slack.

"I won't lose her again."

His gaze darkened and narrowed.

"I won't stop until I have her back," she continued. "You need to understand that."

One dark blond brow arched. "Duly noted. May the best family win." He turned his back and called out over his shoulder. "Let's go, before I change my mind."

Chapter Twelve

Gary warmed up a can of soup while Sophie took a hot shower and changed into a pair of his sweatpants and one of his favorite flannel shirts.

When she emerged from the bathroom, lines of worry and fatigue still edged the corners of her brown eyes.

"Feel any better?"

He regretted the question as soon as he'd asked it. Of course a shower wouldn't make her feel better. Clean? Yes. Better? No. Hell, the woman had just watched her house burn to the ground.

Her only answer was a weak smile. "Smells good out here."

"Chicken noodle," he answered. "My

mother always said a good bowl of soup can cure anything."

Tears glistened in her eyes, but she blinked them away. "Sounds like a plan."

The anger he'd felt after their exchange back at the fire scene began to ease as he watched her expression now. Her look bordered on defeated, on broken. Gary pointed to a chair. "Sit down. I'll get you a bowl."

"Thanks."

Sophie slid into a chair and rolled her neck from side to side, eyes closed.

Gary watched the move as he ladled soup into two large bowls Maggie had given him as part of a dishware set she'd sworn he couldn't live without. He'd never had any reason to use much more than paper plates.

Until now.

He placed a steaming bowl in front of Sophie and handed her a spoon.

She met his gaze and their eyes locked. A frustrating mix of anger and sympathy tangled in his gut. While he admired her determination to get Ally back, she was talking about his niece, damn it. *His* niece. Not hers.

He'd loved Ally for five years. Sophie

hadn't set eyes on the child during that same time. Surely that had to count for something.

Then he reminded himself of the obvious motivation behind her search. She had no one else. No living parents. No living siblings. Apparently no one special in her life.

She'd succeeded in protecting her heart— right into a solitary existence.

Pity simmered inside him, but he tamped it down. Sophie had made her choices. Now she had to live with them. They might have had it all once. Love. Marriage. Children. But she'd walked away.

As much as he'd like to think differently, his most basic instinct told him that, given the chance, she'd make the same choice again.

Even so, he had to do something to ease the pain plastered across her face.

"I know you feel alone right now, but you're not. You have me." His words surprised him, and, based on the quick widening of Sophie's eyes, they'd surprised her as well.

So much for his promise to keep the woman from getting under his skin this time around. He'd let her worm her way in, whether he liked it or not.

"You don't have to worry about me." She shrugged, sipping a spoonful of broth.

But Gary could read the truth in her eyes. Her careful world of protective walls had begun to crumble, and she was scared.

He couldn't remember the last time he'd seen Sophie scared, if ever. "I won't let anything happen to you, even though we're on opposite sides of this thing."

The sadness around her eyes was quickly replaced by a sharp focus. "We both want what's right for Robin."

He met her gaze and held it. "You're assuming she and Ally are one and the same."

Gary looked for a weakening of her stance, but saw none. "I'm right, and you know it." She dropped her focus back to her soup, as if dismissing his attempt at conversation.

So be it. If she wanted to remain antagonistic, he'd be more than happy to do so.

Once he'd secured his family's happiness, he'd be leaving for his new spot in Los Angeles—leaving Sophie Markham and all thoughts of what might have been behind.

He chuckled to himself. Who was he kidding? Even if they both wanted to be together, which wasn't going to happen, people in battle over a child didn't end up together. The emotional price was too high, and the pain of losing would be too raw.

Even love couldn't transcend those wounds.

HOURS LATER, GARY LAY AWAKE. Still. He'd checked on Sophie numerous times during the night and had been surprised to find her sleeping soundly each time. Chalk one up for Mom's soup theory.

He, on the other hand, had remained wide awake, doing his best to sort out the jumble of emotions wreaking havoc on his heart and thoughts. He couldn't afford to let anything sway him from fighting to keep Ally with Maggie. The child was where she belonged—where she was meant to be. End of story.

Yes, Sophie had apparently allowed herself to care—really care—somewhere along the way during the past few days, but that couldn't override the five years of love and nurturing Maggie and Robert had provided.

He mentally chastised himself, realizing he'd already concluded Ally was Robin Markham.

Sophie had been correct in that respect.

Every piece of evidence uncovered might be circumstantial, but each was compelling. The clues fit neatly into the puzzle.

Johnson had murdered Rebecca Markham and used Teresa Cartwright to place Robin for adoption. Then he'd murdered Cartwright and vanished with the adoption fee. The question was where had the man gone? And why had he resurfaced now? What connection did he have that had notified him of Sophie's theory?

Surely someone or something had given him a wake-up call. That was the only way to explain the attacks on Sophie and Robert as well as Franklin's conveniently timed drowning.

The phone rang a little past 6:00 a.m., and Gary pounced on the receiver, not wanting anything to wake Sophie. He wasn't surprised to hear Maggie's voice. She'd been so upset last night after he'd told her about the fire that he imagined she hadn't slept at all.

"I'm leaving." Her words were sure and short, right to the point.

"Leaving where?" He drew in a deep breath, working to make sense of just what it was his sister was saying.

"Leaving South Jersey," she answered. "Leaving the entire region. What if Johnson comes after us? What then?"

A moment of silence stretched between them.

"I'm taking Ally and running." Maggie's voice dropped low. "I can't lose her, Gary. I'd rather run for the rest of my life than lose her."

Gary came fully alert. "Don't do it. If you run they'll hold it against you when it comes to custody."

"She's my daughter." The venom in Maggie's voice was unrecognizable. "I won't let Sophie take her away. I don't care who her birth mother was, I'm her mother. Me. No one else."

Gary tried to corral his frenzied thoughts. He had to keep his sister calm. Had to keep her rational.

"No court is going to take her away from you. You've given her a great life. You love her. She loves you. Anyone can see that." He hesitated for a split second, deciding to ask her to do something he was fairly short on himself. "Have faith."

"Faith?" Maggie's voice climbed several octaves. "I had faith before my son died. I had faith when Robert miraculously showed up with Ally, free and available for placement. I had faith before Sophie Markham threw our lives into turmoil."

Her voice softened, and if Gary wasn't mistaken, his sister was fighting tears. "I had faith before my husband was nearly beaten to death. I don't have *faith* anymore, Gary. It's time to stop praying and start running."

"What about Robert?" Gary asked. "Did you tell him your plan?"

His sister hesitated a bit too long, and Gary realized her next answer was probably a lie.

"I did," she replied. "He told me he'd catch up to us when he's well."

A small twinge of suspicion sprang to life at the base of Gary's brain. "Who else did you tell?"

"No one."

Her answer came too quickly. Someone spoke from behind her. A deep voice. A male voice.

Alarm came to life in Gary's veins.

"Who's with you?"

Her intake of breath sounded crystal-clear across the line. "Trevor James."

Gary muttered a string of expletives. "Just when was it you became incapable of making a decision without that quack's input?"

"I'm hanging up now. I thought my own brother would be a bit more supportive."

"Damn it, Maggie, you're making a mistake—"

But the distinct click of the phone stopped him short. She'd hung up. Just as promised.

Gary scrubbed a hand across his eyes.

Just what he didn't need. Maggie on the run.

Now he had a choice to make.

Tell Sophie about Maggie and give chase, or keep the focus on Kirk Johnson.

He lowered his face to his palms and swore.

He was stuck between a rock and a hard place, but one thing was certain. Maggie would more than likely be easy to find. Kirk Johnson, on the other hand, was proving to be anything but.

Gary blew out a frustrated sigh, knowing he had no choice. He had to keep himself and Sophie focused on Johnson. Once they'd found the man and prevented him from taking any further action, he'd find Maggie and bring her home—together with her daughter—where she belonged.

THE SOUND OF THE RINGING PHONE jostled Sophie from a deep sleep. She hadn't thought it possible to sleep so well after all that had happened, but, as much as she wanted to deny it, she felt safe with Gary. Secure. Knowing he was one room away had allowed her to let down her guard, and she'd slept like a baby.

She was searching around the foot of the bed for the pair of too-big slippers Gary had set out for her, when her line of focus fell on a faded painted frame. She stepped nearer, her breath catching when she recognized the picture.

She and Gary at the school carnival. He sporting a proud smile and she carrying the biggest teddy bear imaginable.

Her heart gave a pang.

Gary had always encouraged her to live spontaneously and experience life.

She picked up the frame and smiled down

at the young faces, remembering that night. She and Gary had made love for the first time. She'd allowed herself to want him, to need him, savoring every second.

A few short weeks later, she'd walked away, scared of how he'd made her feel. Scared of how much she'd grown to depend on him.

Sophie replaced the frame and headed for the bedroom door, easing it open. Gary's voice filtered down the hall to where she stood.

"If you run, they'll hold it against you when it comes to custody."

His words brought her fully awake, jerking her thoughts instantly from the past to the present.

There was only one person he could be talking to.

Maggie.

And if Maggie was about to take Ally and run, Sophie had to do whatever she could to stop her.

She refused to sit back and let the woman disappear with her niece. Not now. Not ever.

Instinctively she looked for her purse, hoping to make a clean getaway while Gary was still on the phone. But she had no purse.

The memories of last night washed over her. She had nothing.

Sophie padded down the hall silently, trying to catch scraps of Gary's conversation. At least he wasn't encouraging his sister to run. Anything but.

"Who else did you tell?"

Sophie didn't wait around to catch any more of Gary's side of the conversation. She spotted his car keys on the counter a few feet behind him, wrapped her fingers carefully around the ring without making a noise then slipped out of the apartment.

She hadn't gone to the bathroom. Hadn't brushed her teeth. Hadn't combed her hair.

At least one thing was certain. In her current state, even Kirk Johnson wouldn't recognize her.

Once outside, she ran to Gary's Mustang. She barely waited for the ignition to catch before she backed the car out of its parking space and took off out of the apartment-building lot.

She needed to get to Maggie Alexander, and fast, but first, she needed to find some clothes. She kept an extra suit at the station.

Always had. You never knew what might happen out in the field.

As she pulled the car onto the highway, headed toward the city, Sophie sent up a silent prayer. Thank goodness for her on-air vanity. Without it, she'd be calling on Maggie Alexander dressed in her brother's beat-up clothing.

GARY NEVER HEARD SOPHIE SNEAK out of the apartment. Matter of fact, he hadn't realized she'd awakened until he'd made eggs and bacon and tapped on the bedroom door to rouse her from sleep.

If they wanted to expand their search for Johnson, they needed to get going.

"Soph?" He tapped again. "Time to get a move on."

When she didn't answer, he eased the door open, the sight of the empty bed hitting him like a sucker punch. When had she left? And why?

He squeezed his eyes shut and turned back toward the kitchen.

Women.

First his sister was about to complicate things by running, and Sophie was still so emotionally unavailable she'd bailed at her first opportunity.

He frowned as he dug into a plate of eggs.

But when had Sophie left? The only time he'd been distracted had been during the call from Maggie.

His stomach balled into a tight knot.

Had she overheard?

He glanced from where he'd been sitting to the bedroom door. The prospect was a distinct possibility, but Sophie wasn't one to avoid confrontation.

If she'd overheard him telling Maggie not to leave town, Sophie would have questioned him head-on. After all, it was what they paid her the big bucks for.

He shook his head. He couldn't take the chance he might be wrong. Johnson had tried to kill her just hours earlier, and Gary needed to know where she'd gone.

He picked up the phone to dial her number, then realized she no longer had a number, at least not a working one. He dialed Maggie's number instead. If Sophie had overheard his call, she'd have wasted no time in getting to his sister's home.

When Maggie didn't answer, he frowned. His sister lived for her social connections. Even if she was on the other line, she never ignored her Caller ID. Of course, she'd been angry enough with him that she would ignore an incoming call from his number.

He next tried the television station, but an assistant merely told him Sophie was out on leave.

Gary had no sooner pressed the disconnect button than the phone rang.

"Soph?" he asked as he answered.

A male chuckle slid across the line. "Lose another one, Barksdale?"

He recognized Simpson's voice instantly. "What have you got for me?"

"Well—" Simpson paused dramatically "—no one seems to be able to find your guy Johnson. I'm not sure I've ever seen someone disappear so thoroughly, but I did find one little bit of information. This, you're going to love."

Anticipation rippled through Gary and he straightened. "What is it?"

"You owe me big time, buddy."

Impatience edged Gary's anticipation aside. "Whatever. What do you have?"

Simpson dropped his voice low. "You know how they say everyone has a mother?"

Gary brightened, hoping Simpson was about to say what he thought. "Yeah."

"Well, I just found Johnson's. And better yet, I found her phone number."

Gary was out of his chair and heading for his car keys before Simpson finished his sentence. "I'll be right there."

But when his gaze landed on the empty counter, the spot where he always dropped the keys to his Mustang, he swore under his breath.

Not only had Sophie run. This time, she'd taken his car.

Chapter Thirteen

Sophie shouldn't have been surprised when Trevor James answered the door at the Alexander home, but she was. She'd hoped to find Maggie alone, hoped to have a civil conversation, hoped to prevent the woman from running with Ally.

Instead, Sophie found herself studying the smug expression of Maggie's self-help guru.

As usual, the man's hair fell so perfectly into neatly clipped layers Sophie longed to touch the strands simply to prove to herself whether or not his hair was real.

The man was a study in practiced perfection, but then, why shouldn't he be? His perfection had been exactly what had made him rich. He possessed an air of success others wanted to emulate. And the movers and shakers of the Philadelphia region paid a pretty penny to do so.

Sophie refocused on James. His gaze seemed to look through her, rather than at her. She struggled with the sense of a memory trying to emerge from the recesses of her mind.

A shiver whispered up her spine and she blinked. Just who was it this man reminded her of?

When her gaze fell to a pair of matching suitcases sitting at the bottom of the center staircase, all thoughts of Trevor James flew out of her mind.

Her attention shifted solely to preventing Maggie from disappearing.

"Where's Maggie?"

She moved to brush past James, but he grasped her shoulder a bit too firmly and she winced.

"There's no need to get rough."

One calm eyebrow arched. "Isn't there?"

Trevor's tone sent her stomach lurching sideways. He sounded different today. Not his usual pumped-up, motivational self. Instead he sounded…cold…as if all of his usual emotion had left his body.

Sophie ignored her thoughts, retraining her attention on the issue at hand.

She tilted her head toward the suitcases. "I'm not stupid. I can see she's planning to leave and take Ally with her. I can't permit that.

"Maggie?" Sophie paused for a split second after she called out the name. No answer. "Ally?"

Silence.

Where were they?

Again, she moved to pass him, but James forcibly blocked her path, this time sending her careening into the wall.

Sophie swallowed, fear kicking to life in her belly. Her pulse quickened, and she focused on her breathing and her thinking.

There had to be a perfectly logical explanation for the man's behavior. Perfectly logical. She just needed to wrap her brain around what that was.

She stood her ground but scanned the length of the center hall, listening for a sound, looking for a clue as to exactly what was going on.

Her gaze landed on a fire extinguisher tucked next to the telephone stand. Her fire extinguisher—complete with the piece of masking tape she'd marked with the purchase date.

The fear she'd been battling took on a whole new dimension. Had Maggie set the fire at her house? Or used James to do so?

Sophie spun on the man. "Where is she?"

The man said nothing, merely narrowing his gaze.

Sophie jerked her thumb toward the extinguisher. "That came from my house. My house that burnt to the ground last night. I don't suppose you know anything about that, do you?"

Again, James stood silent, his stare never leaving her face.

"Did you advise her on that? Tell her it was the only way to shut me up? Or did you help her? Did you set it together?"

Sophie's typically cool demeanor had vanished, and for once in her life she didn't care how she appeared. Waves of emotion splashed over her—fear, anger, disbelief, hurt. For the first time in a long time she allowed herself to feel, and although the sensation was painful, it was real.

"Pretty convenient," she continued, "rigging a copycat of the other fires."

Something shifted in James's face just then. His stern features eased, one corner of his mouth lifting into a smile. A smile that sent ice crashing through Sophie's veins.

So she'd been right. The fire had been part of a plot to send her running away from the phantom Johnson instead of coming after Ally.

Well, they'd certainly underestimated her.

"I'm calling the police."

This time when she moved to push past James, he let her go. She reached the telephone stand in two steps, but when Sophie plucked the phone from its base nothing but dead air filled her ear. The shiver that had been hovering along her spine spread upward and outward, covering her neck and shoulders.

Why would Maggie cut her own phone line? Unless *she* hadn't cut it at all.

Sophie turned once more to face James. The man had closed the space between them and now stood almost toe to toe with her.

"Where is she?" Sophie pushed the words past her growing trepidation.

James leaned close and Sophie found herself studying his eyes once more.

"She's where she needs to be," he said.

Sophie straightened. "That sounds like one of your own quotes."

The man's eerie smile spread wider. "Matter of fact, it is." He tipped back his head, belly laughing.

The sound set Sophie's teeth on edge, but she seized the opportunity, reversing her steps and cutting through the sitting room, headed straight for the living room.

That's where she found them. Maggie and Ally. Bound and gagged.

Sophie choked on her fear, but pressed forward, moving to reach the apparently unconscious Ally just as the weight of James's blow hit her back, sending her crashing to the hardwood floor.

Countless thoughts whirled through her brain, fighting for position, but as she rolled, struggling to put distance between herself and her attacker, her gaze landed on Trevor James's feet.

His paint-spattered boots.

I was about to get beaten within an inch of

my life, and there I was staring at the guy's feet. Cook's words echoed in her head.

A smiley face.

There it was. Plain as day.

Terror washed over her.

Could Trevor James have been behind everything that had happened? He'd been at Maggie's house the first time Sophie and Gary had argued about Ally, but why on earth would he care? What business of his was any of this?

He leaned over her, snarling. "You never could keep your nose out of trouble, could you?"

His tone of voice had changed—the pitch, the intonation, the accent.

This time, when Sophie looked up into Trevor James's eyes, she recognized him for who he really was.

It took only a split second for her memory to provide every answer she sought.

Bile clawed at her throat and she choked it down.

There was no time to panic, no time to feel fear. If she wanted to get out of this alive *and* save Maggie and Ally, she had to think fast—faster than the man behind those eyes.

She sent up a silent prayer and worked to calm the frantic beating of her heart.

God help her.

IT TOOK GARY OVER FORTY-FIVE minutes to reach the office. He'd had to walk to the train station, then change lines in midtown to reach the *Inquirer* office.

He wasn't sure exactly what Sophie's game was, but at this point, he didn't care. His days of worrying about Sophie Markham and her tightly wound emotions were over.

Simpson rose to his feet as soon as Gary entered the newsroom. He nonchalantly walked past Gary's desk and dropped a folded sheet of paper onto the mess of notes and folders covering the work space.

Their gazes locked and Gary nodded, saying nothing.

He waited a few moments before he unfolded the paper, reading the notations Simpson had made.

Martha Johnson.

Gary scanned the phone number, trying to place the area code as he dialed. His best guess was somewhere on the West Coast.

He listened as the woman's phone rang. Once. Twice. Three times. Her machine picked up on the fourth ring.

Disappointment and urgency welled inside him as he left his message. He needed to find Johnson and the man's mother was the first solid lead they had.

Years of experience as a reporter told him the woman wasn't likely to return his call, so his message included a white lie. He said he was a friend of a friend and had found some money owed to Kirk.

Money did funny things to people, even parents.

Perhaps if he was lucky, Martha Johnson would take the bait and return his call. Twenty minutes later, she did just that.

"Mr. Barksdale?" The woman's voice was tentative yet steady. "I'm afraid I can't help you find my son. He and I haven't kept in touch, but I didn't want to leave you hanging."

Someone with a conscience. Hope bubbled inside Gary. Johnson's mother might be just what he needed to unlock the truth behind the man's vanishing act.

"Maybe you could tell me a little more

about him then?" Gary probed carefully, wanting to remain subtle, yet fervently longing to get to the meat of the conversation.

He let his reporter instincts take over, gently guiding the content of their talk to the points that mattered.

"I thought you knew my son?" Johnson asked, skepticism edging into her voice.

"I'm afraid I don't, ma'am. I'm a friend of a friend, but I'd like to understand your son."

A dejected sigh sounded on the other end of the line. "I don't believe anyone can understand my son, young man."

Gary seized the opportunity to come clean.

"Ma'am, I know about your son's violent past."

Martha Johnson gasped.

"And now he's threatened my family. Would you please help me?"

"I thought you said you had money for him?"

"I lied, ma'am. I lied to get you to call me back."

Several awkward seconds of silence stretched between them. Finally, Johnson spoke.

"I don't think a mother can ever come to

terms with bringing such a monster into this world."

Gary straightened, startled by the woman's comment. For once in his life, he found himself at a loss for words. "I'm sorry."

"Don't be," she continued. "I stopped feeling sorry for myself a long time ago. When he vanished, I picked up and moved out here. I figured the farther, the better."

Gary said nothing, realizing the woman welcomed the opportunity to talk to someone.

"I'm sorry for your family's trouble. My advice would be for them to get as far away from my son as quickly as they can."

"When did you first worry he might be dangerous?" Gary asked.

"Too late, I'm afraid. I should have seen the warning signs when he was small, but I didn't." Her deep sigh sounded clearly across the line. "It was all textbook, now that I've read the textbooks." She chuckled, the sound bitter and short.

"He injured neighborhood pets. He set fires. He was just…absent emotionally."

If Gary wasn't mistaken, the poor woman was on the verge of tears.

"I never believed him capable of harming people," she continued. "He was just a sad, confused boy."

Gary chose that moment to dig deeper. "Do you feel he was wrongly convicted for your parents' deaths? Do you think the fire was an accident?"

More silence beat between them, then Martha answered.

"No. My parents had tried to discipline him in the past. They thought they could help. I'd gone away for the weekend— I needed a break—they offered to take Kirk for me."

Emotion choked her voice. "I never saw them again. They say he set the fire while they slept.

"I thought once he spent all that time in juvenile detention things would be different, but when he came home, he seemed more evil. I hadn't thought that possible.

"Can you imagine what it's like to be terrified of your own son, Mr. Barksdale?"

Gary shook his head. "No, ma'am. I can't."

"It's horrible." Martha's voice was barely a whisper now. "When he announced he was leaving home, I threw out most everything he'd left behind and I moved." She laughed again. "I thought distance would make me forget the pain. What a fool I was."

"So you have no idea where he went or where he might be living now?"

"I haven't heard from my son in five years."

Since the time of Ally's adoption and Teresa Cartwright's death.

Gary seized on another of Johnson's statements, and a twinge of adrenaline kicked to life in his veins.

"You said you threw out most everything he'd left behind, Mrs. Johnson. May I ask what you didn't throw away? Maybe there's something there that will help me find him in time to protect my family."

Her sharp intake of breath rattled in his ear. "I don't really know why I kept it...." Her voice trailed off, then picked up steam once again. "Maybe I thought I needed a reminder of just how sick Kirk was, as if I could ever forget."

Gary reined in his excitement, his gut telling him whatever Martha Johnson had kept might be key. "What is it, Mrs. Johnson?"

"He created a face."

"A face?" Disbelief edged out his hope. What good could a piece of art do for his investigation?

"He cut out pictures from magazines," she continued. "Eyes, lips, a nose, even hair. He pasted them all on a sheet of paper to make a face. I always wondered if he didn't know how evil he was deep down inside, as if a new image might help him hide from his own reflection."

Gary squeezed his eyes shut. "And you still have this picture, Mrs. Johnson?"

"Oh, it's somewhere around here, I suppose. I finally packed it away out of sight years ago."

Gary drew in a deep breath. "I don't suppose you might have access to a fax machine?"

He could practically hear her frown, then she made a snapping noise with her mouth. "I think Mildred Jones has one next door. She uses it for that makeup business she runs."

Gary chose his words thoughtfully, not wanting to push too hard, but needing the woman's full cooperation. "If there's any way you could fax a copy to me, I'd sure appreciate it."

"You're not out to rile up my son, are you?" Martha's voice had climbed to a warning tone. "He's best left alone."

"No, ma'am, you have my word. I just want to protect my loved ones." Gary held his breath, hoping his last sentence would hit home.

"Give me your number." Johnson spoke softly. "I'll see what I can do."

A full half hour later, Gary's pacing at the newsroom's facsimile machine paid off. An incoming number with the same area code as Martha Johnson's displayed in the machine's window.

He held his breath, knowing the collage was probably going to be nothing more than a crazy manifestation of a crazy mind.

As the sheet emerged and he let it slide onto his palm, nothing could have prepared him for what he saw.

Nothing.

The room spun and Gary gripped the table to steady himself.

The image he held in his hand explained how someone like Johnson could so fully disappear. He'd recreated himself.

He'd recreated himself and reinvented his

life, growing rich along the way by manipulating others.

"Hey, anything come through yet?" Simpson's voice sounded just over his shoulder.

Gary turned to meet his friend's questioning gaze, pointing to the sheet of paper.

"Sonofa—"

"Exactly," Gary cut Simpson short.

He returned his attention to the face created by the combination of carefully chosen features, amazed at the likeness.

Trevor James.

The self-proclaimed life coach to the rich and famous of the Philadelphia region. A man in whom his sister had placed all of her trust. A man with everything to lose and nothing to gain if his violent past became public knowledge.

He no doubt would stop at nothing to keep his true identity a secret.

The magnitude of what he'd uncovered hit Gary full-force.

He had to reach Maggie, had to tell her to get the hell away from James.

"Let's keep a lid on this for now," he urged Simpson as he headed for his desk.

Gary dialed Maggie's number as quickly as he could, praying he wasn't too late.

Trevor James had obviously told her to run in order to eliminate the last possible trace of evidence linking him to his chain of crimes—and his past.

Ally.

Gary's heart twisted.

If James had hurt one hair on Ally's head, he'd kill the man.

Maggie's phone rang and rang and rang. No answer. Now was not the time for her to ignore him.

Sweat broke out on Gary's palms and he wiped his hands against his jeans.

Dread pooled in his stomach, pulsing like a living, breathing thing.

Something was wrong. Very wrong. And if Sophie *had* overheard his conversation with Maggie, chances were she had walked into whatever trap James had set at his sister's home.

Simpson now stood next to his desk, brows furrowed.

Gary had to move, and he had to move fast.

"I need you to call in a favor with your

buddy on the force." Gary's pulse roared in his ears as he spoke the words. He jotted down Maggie's address and handed it to his coworker. "Ask him to get there quick and silent. I think she's in danger."

Simpson nodded, taking the slip of paper and reaching for Gary's phone.

"One more thing."

Simpson lifted his gaze, eyes wide.

Gary dropped his voice low, intent. "I need to borrow your car."

Chapter Fourteen

Sophie looked up into the face of Trevor James, but focused on his eyes. His dead eyes.

Was it possible? Could it be? But how?

"You always thought you were so smart, didn't you?"

His accent came through now. Not the voice of the supposedly sophisticated man he'd somehow become, but the low-life intonation of the evil man he'd once been and evidently still was.

Raw terror sliced through every inch of Sophie's body. She'd give anything to jump to her feet and run, but she couldn't, not if her escape meant leaving Maggie and Ally behind.

"Kirk?" She didn't recognize her own voice, so tight with fear it sounded as though it came from somewhere else—someone else.

The man nodded, the evil in his eyes taking on a satisfied glint.

"How did you—?"

"Lots of money and lots of plastic surgery," he answered the question before Sophie had finished asking it. "It's amazing what you can achieve when you put your mind to it."

A bone-chilling grin tugged at one corner of his mouth. "Another of my sayings, in case you're keeping track."

Maggie made a strangled sound from behind the duct tape that covered her mouth.

James tipped his chin in Maggie's direction. "One of my best students as well as one of my best-paying."

Sophie scrambled to a sitting position, scooting closer to where Maggie and Ally were. Her gaze landed on the fireplace, the hearth, the rack of wrought-iron tools.

She quickly refocused on James, not wanting him to realize what she'd spotted.

"Why don't you let them go?" Sophie asked. "Isn't it me you'd like to stop?"

One brow lifted. "Oh, I'll stop you. Just like I stopped your sister."

He leaned down close, his breath brushing her face. She cringed.

"You, Maggie and Ally are the last remaining pieces of evidence against me. Evidence of who I really am."

He narrowed his gaze, eyeing her as if he couldn't believe how stupid she was. "Don't you see? Once you're gone, no one can stop me."

"Gary will." Sophie spoke the words with nothing but confidence, knowing she spoke the truth.

Gary *would* stop this man.

He'd no doubt search the ends of the earth to bring James down if anything happened to his sister or niece.

A moment of sadness flashed through her when she realized Gary probably wouldn't do the same for her. She wished he would, she realized, letting herself feel honest emotion for once.

What a pathetic soul she was. Faced with apparent death, she was suddenly ready to own up to the emotions Gary had consistently challenged her to feel.

She'd never get the chance to tell him.

Unless she fought like hell.

First, she had to keep James talking. As long as he didn't realize her efforts were a ploy for more time, she had no doubt he'd revel in the chance to detail his brilliant atrocities.

Hell, he'd gotten rich simply by talking; why would he go silent now?

"Why did you kill Becca?" The words were difficult to articulate, as if asking the question was the final validation that her sister's death had been no accident.

Sophie had been correct about getting James to explain himself. The man brightened at the question.

"She knew who I was."

"Who were you?" Sophie urged him to continue, stealing a glance at Maggie's wide, terrified eyes. Ally's eyes were open now and equally as terrified as her mother's.

Poor sweet girl. Sophie's heart ached. Ally didn't deserve any of this. Not a blessed second.

For a split second, Cook's voice sounded in her brain.

What if what's right is leaving that girl where she is?

Sophie realized she'd caused every second of this suffering with her theories, her questions, her refusal to leave Ally's parentage alone. Regret swelled inside her.

James squatted down now, obviously enjoying the give-and-take. Sophie took the opportunity to move a few inches backward, closer to the rack of fireplace tools and the heavy, iron poker.

"I was not a kind child," James answered. "I once set a fire that killed my grandparents."

Another muffled cry came from Maggie, and James shot her a frown.

"Why?" Sophie asked.

He turned back to face her, tilting his head sideways. "Why did I kill them? Or why did I set the fire?"

Sophie nodded, her mind seizing on the obvious. The man was insane. She could hear it in his voice, see it in his eyes, feel it in his past.

James shrugged and gave a low chuckle. "Because they had it coming, of course. What other reason would there be?"

Anger began to push at the terror inside Sophie.

"What about Becca? Did she have it coming, too?"

He nodded. "When I refused to leave, she used a friend to pull up my juvenile record. She threatened to expose me if I didn't leave her alone."

Sophie drew in a steadying breath, taking another imperceptible move back. "So why not leave her alone?"

"No one threatens me and lives."

Something shifted now in James's eyes, in his tone. The polished motivational-speaker intonations took over once more, edging out the boy he'd obviously worked very hard to leave far behind.

"So you did kill her?"

James pursed his lips. "Strangled her. Set the fire to cover it up. Worked beautifully."

Sadness flooded through Sophie. If only she'd done more to save her sister, to keep her safe. If only she'd dug deeper after the fire. Maybe she'd have uncovered the truth five years ago and saved everyone involved from the additional suffering.

"And Robin?" she asked.

"I left her to die."

He spoke the words so coolly, so flatly, that Sophie gagged. Grief gripped her.

"She's dead?"

"Not yet." James shook his head. "My girlfriend heard her cry and went into the house to save her." He laughed. "She wanted to keep her. Can you imagine?"

He grimaced as if the thought was unthinkable. "Like I would ever want a child around."

Sophie breathed in slowly, making another move toward the fireplace. This time, her fingertips brushed the edge of the brick hearth.

She was getting closer. A few more maneuvers and she'd be in position.

Maggie made a sudden motion, drawing James's focus to her. Sophie made a second move.

When he retrained his focus on Sophie, she pressed her lips together as if trying to appreciate everything he'd said.

"Was that Teresa Cartwright?" she asked.

James nodded. "I sent her to my old friend Franklin. I knew he'd take care of the adoption, and keep quiet. I trusted him. I told her to pose as the birth mother, and he never asked any questions."

He smiled again, the cold, satisfied smile of a madman. "The placement and the money were far easier than I'd anticipated."

"Brian Franklin had defended you after you killed your grandparents, correct?"

James's brows lifted once more. "You've been doing your homework, I see."

"It's why I make the big bucks." Sophie's flippant tone belied the disgust she felt inside each time James opened his mouth to speak.

"Don't be smart," he warned. "Teresa thought she was smart. She thought she could trick me into a marriage proposal in return for placing the baby. She was dead wrong."

Sophie decided to push him. "So, when you killed Teresa in exactly the same way you'd killed Becca, you didn't worry about getting caught?"

"I disappeared the next day." He shrugged. "Who was going to find me?"

"I have to commend you on that." Sophie shook her head. "Even with all the resources I have, I couldn't find a trace of you after that date. It was as if you vanished."

She stared at him, studying his features—

the features that had been created by a surgeon's knife.

"Kirk Johnson vanished," James replied. "Trevor James was born."

"And did quite well for himself."

"When you've got a talent for manipulation, why not use it?" His smug expression sickened her. "After all, everyone knows the nice guy finishes last."

Sophie pressed on. "I'd say you did well enough that you'd do just about anything to preserve your reputation—" she gestured toward his face "—your identity."

His eyes grew colder. Sophie hadn't thought it possible. "I'd be foolish not to."

"Is that why you took on Maggie as a client?"

James pursed his lips, as if the memory pleased him. "She was a natural student, and I so enjoy control. Why not use my skills to manipulate her while I kept tabs on the child's whereabouts?"

"The attack on Robert?" Sophie asked.

"A warning and an opportunity to take the original placement paperwork from his office."

She shook her head. "But all he knew was

your name. Kirk Johnson. He thought you referred Teresa, nothing more. What threat was he to you?"

"A connection. I don't like connections."

"What about me?" Sophie gave a quick lift and drop of her shoulders. "You were the one who attacked me, weren't you?"

"I thought another attack on a well-known reporter might slow you down." His brows lifted. "Alas, even I make mistakes."

"What about my cameraman? He posed no threat to you?"

"Collateral damage."

"Franklin?"

Sophie's questions came rapid-fire now, her reporter's brain having kicked into high gear. The man had been quite brilliant in his thought processes, leaving no possible tie to himself intact.

Her heart pounded in her throat. She needed only one more move to reach the poker—one more move to knock the man out of commission and get Maggie and Ally to safety.

Maggie jerked her body again. This time, Trevor stepped toward her, reaching to check the rope he'd secured around her ankles and wrists.

Sophie made her move.

In one fluid motion, she grabbed the poker from the rack of tools on the hearth, lunging toward James and swinging.

He never knew what hit him. The wrought iron connected with the back of his head, sending him reeling forward. He caught himself on the edge of a credenza, holding his body upright for what seemed like the longest moment of Sophie's life.

Then he turned to face her, his hatred pure and blatant in his eyes before he slumped, crumpling onto the floor.

A shudder ripped through Sophie and she held her breath.

Trevor James stayed down.

Disbelief washed over her. Could it really be over? Had the mighty man fallen with just one blow?

She scrambled to where Maggie and Ally sat, making a move to untie Maggie's hands. The woman cut her eyes at Ally, and Sophie instinctively moved toward the little girl, fumbling with the knots securing her ropes.

When they finally eased open, she slid the bonds from Ally's slender wrists and ankles. Her skin had been chafed bright red and raw, and Sophie knew with absolute certainty she'd make James pay dearly for all of the pain he'd inflicted, all of the lives he'd damaged or destroyed.

She took Ally's face in her hands and stared into her eyes. "Run, honey. Get out of the house."

Ally hesitated, navy eyes huge with fear. "Mommy."

Sophie's heart was in her throat. "Mommy's coming, honey, I promise. But she needs you to run. Run next door and hide."

James stirred, pulling himself to a kneeling position. Sophie's stomach lurched and she saw matching fear painted across Maggie's face.

Damn. So much for her bravado at having beat him. She had to get Ally out of harm's way and out of the house now.

The man's complexion had gone scarlet with rage, and Sophie knew they'd all pay the consequences of her having struck him down.

"Now!" she screamed at Ally, pushing the girl toward the door.

James scrambled to his feet, capturing Ally in his arms.

The little girl squealed, but James only laughed.

"Once she's dead, there will be nothing to tie me to any of this. Nothing."

Sophie's insides rolled. The man was set on killing his own daughter. If that wasn't pure evil, she didn't know what was. Before she had time to do anything, Maggie acted.

Even though bound and gagged, Maggie hurtled herself at James, careening into his side and knocking him to the hard floor. Ally scrambled free, but reached for her mommy.

Maggie shook her head, jerking her chin toward the kitchen.

Ally hesitated, tears streaming down her cheeks, her innocent eyes bright with fear and uncertainty.

"Please, Ally," Sophie begged. "Go now, honey. Go!"

The girl disappeared around the doorway just as James climbed to his feet, backhanding

Maggie. She fell headlong into the edge of an end table then slumped to the floor, lifeless.

"No," Sophie murmured under her breath.

Bright red blood spread from the head wound.

She'd risked her life to save her child. Thrown herself physically between her daughter and the man who wanted her dead.

Her daughter. Ally truly was Maggie's daughter, and Maggie had done what any loving mother would. She'd fought for her child's life.

Something Sophie's own mother had never done.

When she realized how long she'd been staring at Maggie, Sophie pivoted, raising her hands defensively, knowing James surely would come after her next.

The man did not disappoint.

Only this time, it was he who held the fireplace poker.

GARY CAREENED SIMPSON'S CAR around the corner of Maggie's street, tires squealing in the typically quiet residential neighborhood.

There were no signs of police activity

when he pulled up front, launching himself from the car in a full-out sprint.

So much for calling in the cavalry.

Since he'd left the office, Gary had been ringing his sister's phone continuously with no luck. Hell, he'd even tried Sophie's cell on the off-chance she'd replaced the phone already. Yet all of his efforts had been in vain.

His heart caught at the sight of his Mustang parked at the curb, confirming his fear Sophie had walked in on whatever James had planned.

He could only hope he wasn't too late to stop the man from whatever it was he intended to do.

Not wanting to waste any time, Gary dashed around the side of the house toward the kitchen door—the door Maggie always left unlocked even though he and Robert had told her countless times to be more careful.

He had his hand on the knob when he heard a whimper.

Then another.

Then a sob.

He instantly recognized the small, scared voice.

"Ally?" Gary froze in his tracks, listening.

He waited for the next cry, moving closer to Ally when it sounded. He repeated the process until he found her, knees pulled to her chest, tears streaming down her face, hidden behind one of Maggie's favorite azalea bushes.

Pure fear twisted her features, but she quickly relaxed, reaching for him when she saw him.

Anxious concern pounded in Gary's chest, and his heart ached at the terror etched on his little niece's face. Anger and sympathy tangled in his gut as he reached for her, pulling her into his arms and clutching her tightly.

"I've got you, honey. Uncle Gary's here." He whispered against her hair, hoping his soothing tone would calm her crying, now punctuated by hiccups. "Are you hurt?"

Ally shook her head.

"Where's Mommy?"

"In heaven." Ally pushed the words around a hiccup and Gary's stomach roiled.

"Heaven?"

"He knocked her down and she hit her head. She had a boo-boo."

Gary took a deep breath in through his

nose, fighting to maintain his composure for his niece's benefit. "Just because she has a boo-boo doesn't mean she's in heaven."

Her eyes widened hopefully and he did his best to give her a reassuring smile.

"Who hit Mommy, Ally?" Even though his gut knew, he wanted to hear it from someone who had been inside the house.

"Her friend." Ally's huge eyes swam with tears, and rage filled Gary.

"Mommy's friend who comes over all the time? Mr. James?"

Ally nodded and Gary swore inwardly. So help him God, he'd kill Johnson...James— whatever persona he was today—with his bare hands, if he'd harmed Maggie or Sophie.

He had to move quickly. Had to get Ally to safety and then find Maggie and Sophie.

"How'd you get out here, honey?"

"The lollipop lady. She untied me and told me to run."

Untied her? Gary winced. Violence of the sort he knew Kirk Johnson capable of was something no five-year-old should have to witness.

He refused to believe Maggie was dead.

Refused. But what about Sophie? His throat tightened, and he realized he could no longer deny the depth of feeling he held for the woman.

He could tell himself he wanted to take the job in Los Angeles, tell himself he didn't care about Sophie and her stifled emotions, but he'd be lying.

He more than cared for her. If he didn't know better, he'd swear he—

"The lollipop lady hit Mr. James."

Ally's words interrupted Gary's thoughts.

So Sophie had fought back. *Thank God.*

Now he just had to reach her and get her out of there. But first, he had to get Ally safely tucked away, where James couldn't find her.

He bundled her more tightly into his arms and hurried back down the sidewalk.

"She told me to go next door."

"Who, honey?"

"The lollipop lady."

Gary nodded. "Then that's what we'll do."

"What about Mommy? Will you fix her boo-boo, Uncle Gary?"

Ally's sobbing started again, and Gary's heart caught in his chest. He dropped a kiss to her cheek and gave her a squeeze. "I'll take good care of her for you. I promise."

He only hoped he hadn't just made a promise he couldn't keep.

Gary crossed to the next-door neighbor's house, and pounded on the side door. A startled-looking woman opened the door a moment later, and he foisted Ally into her arms.

"Call 911, and don't let anyone touch her. Not anyone."

The woman nodded, apparently too stunned to speak, but Gary was already headed back toward Maggie's house.

There was no time to wait for the police.

A familiar acrid smell teased at his nostrils as he pushed through the kitchen door. Gary's gut tightened with dread.

Fire.

The memory of the smell was all too fresh from the night before.

Fingers of smoke licked at the kitchen doorway, and Gary held his breath as he raced forward, not knowing what he was about to find, but praying he wasn't too late to save the two most important women in his life.

His sister.
And the woman he'd grown to love.
Again.

Chapter Fifteen

James swung and Sophie ducked, taking a glancing blow on her shoulder.

Concentrate. She had to shove down any doubts about her survival and concentrate— simply concentrate.

It was up to her to get herself and Maggie out of this ordeal alive. Up to her to find Ally and get her as far away from James as possible, before he had a chance to eliminate his last *connections*.

The monster.

She'd taken countless self-defense classes, covered countless stories in which women described how they'd fought off their attackers.

If there was ever a time to draw on what she knew, this was it.

James swore loudly and raised the wrought-iron poker again. Sophie dove out of the way, rolling toward the hearth and the rack of remaining tools.

Two could play at this game.

She grabbed at the first object she could reach, wrapping her fingers around the cool metal handle. She raised her weapon to fend off James's glancing blow, swearing softly when she realized she wielded nothing more than a small broom.

No matter. It was something, and something was a whole lot better than the nothing she'd held in her hands the moment before.

They circled each other and James smiled.

"You must be joking." He made a clucking noise with his mouth. "You would have been perfect for my services. I could have worked wonders with a woman who thinks she can beat a man like me with a broom.

"It's a shame I have to kill you. You might have been my prized pupil."

He cast a glance at Maggie's lifeless body.

"It seems my current prized pupil might be permanently out of commission."

Sophie hated the man in that moment.

Out and out hated him.

She'd never physically harmed another person, but she knew she would harm James, given the chance. The depth of the rage that filled her stunned her, yet energized her.

Adrenaline pumped through her veins and she focused, trying to anticipate his next move.

James raised the poker and moved to strike her, but when Sophie shifted to a defensive position, James twisted, altering the direction of his swing, landing a solid blow to her ribs.

Pain exploded out from the point of impact, matching the panic exploding inside her.

She couldn't let him win. Couldn't.

Concentrate.

If she kept making mistakes, he'd overpower her in no time.

He moved toward her, cold eyes glistening with evil. Sophie backed away from him, keeping the space between them steady.

Shock gripped her when her heel came against a solid object. She stumbled, struggling to keep her balance, but tripping, falling.

She completely lost her balance and hit the floor. Hard.

Sophie found herself face-to-face with Maggie. Still bleeding. Pale as a ghost.

She winced. She'd fallen right over the poor thing.

"Hang on," Sophie said softly. "I'm getting us out of this."

"You're not getting the two of you out of anything."

Sophie scrambled to her knees, but James was already on top of her, pressing her to the floor with the heel of his boot. His paint-spattered boots.

"You didn't get your sister out of anything with your little restraining order."

His words ripped the old emotional wound wide open. He was right. She'd failed Becca.

"Maybe you can tell her you're sorry once you're dead."

Sophie's intestines turned to liquid and she squeezed her eyes shut.

She'd often wondered how she might die. Morbid, yes, but after losing a mother to suicide and the rest of her family to the house fire, death had frequently occupied much of her thoughts.

But one thing was different now.

Now, she wanted to live.

She'd never quite felt that desire before. She'd never had the urge to harm herself, but she'd also never been passionate about life.

That had changed during the past week.

That had changed because of Ally, and that had changed because of Gary.

Seeing him again, being with him again, had brought her back to life.

She liked how he challenged her—needed how he challenged her.

She needed him.

The thought didn't terrify her as it once had, but the thought of dying before she could tell him did.

Sophie struggled furiously against James, but he'd now pinned her with his knee and bound her hands behind her. He ripped off a length of duct tape and slapped it over her mouth, grinning as he did so.

He finished by anchoring her ankles together. When he rolled Sophie next to Maggie, Sophie thought he might leave the room, might give her time to struggle against her bonds, but she was mistaken.

James moved around the room, pouring

something from a small container he'd plucked from a corner.

A chemical smell tickled her nose. When her understanding of what he was doing clicked into focus, she shuddered, her mouth going bone dry.

He meant to burn them alive, covering his crime just as he'd done with Becca and Teresa Cartwright.

"You're not so smart now, are you?" His voice had taken on a hysterical note, as if he were overexcited by everything that had happened.

"I'm always amazed at how easy this part is," he continued. "Did you know fire was my first love?"

Sophie felt her eyes go huge as he methodically spread whatever it was he used, then struck a match.

"Fire is the only thing that never disappoints."

He looked at her then, and Sophie realized his eyes weren't only dead, they were vacant. The man possessed no soul. He couldn't. Not to be able to do the horrible things he'd done.

"I'm going to light this now and then you'll die." He shrugged. "Just like your sister and just like Teresa." He made a snapping noise with his mouth. "I had to use water for Franklin. Shoving him over the side of the boat wasn't very challenging. Bit of a disappointment actually."

He dropped the match and the accelerant ignited with a whoosh.

James stood over Sophie one last time, pushing against her ribs with the toe of his boot.

"If you'll excuse me, I've got to go find my daughter. I should have let her die the first time I had the chance."

He was gone before the impact of his words fully hit Sophie.

Ally.

She didn't deserve to die at the hands of the madman, her own flesh and blood, her own father. She didn't deserve to die at all.

Sophie willed her brain to find a solution, to find a way out of this horror show.

She had to fight. Had to fight to stop Trevor James before he could lay one finger on that beautiful, innocent little girl.

But as the flames lapped along the baseboard and ignited the stylish paisley drapes Maggie had obviously so carefully hung, Sophie's hope dimmed.

What she and Maggie needed now was nothing short of a miracle.

THE SMOKE AND HEAT THICKENED as Gary made his way down the hall. Instinctively, he headed for the living room. Anytime he'd seen Trevor James at this house, he'd been in this room with Maggie.

Chances were the man had stayed within familiar territory today.

His heart stopped at the intensity of the blazing fire inside and the sight of two bodies on the floor. When one body rolled—seemingly trying to protect the other—he sprang into action, pulling her away, dragging her toward the hall.

He recognized the short dark hair, the determined expression. Sophie fought him momentarily, until she recognized him.

Her features crumpled into tears of relief just before he yanked the duct tape from her face.

"Get Maggie," she pleaded. "She's badly hurt. Get her out."

Gary fumbled with the rope at her ankles, sending up a silent thank-you when the knot easily slipped free. He pulled her to her feet and shoved her toward the kitchen.

"Go."

She hesitated, her gaze locking with his, her gratitude and desperation blatant in her eyes.

"Go!"

He shouted the word as he bundled his sister into his arms. This time, Sophie listened, racing ahead of him down the hall toward the promise of fresh air just outside the back door.

Sirens wailed and emergency vehicles filled the street as they cleared the threshold.

"About time," Gary muttered under his breath.

Two rescue personnel sprinted toward him, taking Maggie from him and rushing her toward a waiting vehicle.

He turned, looking for Sophie. She'd dropped to the grass a distance from the house, hands still bound. He moved to where she sat, squatting in front of her.

He freed her wrists, then cupped her chin with his hand, pulling her into a quick kiss.

He kept a firm grip on her face and he looked into her eyes.

She'd more than gotten under his skin this time around. This time, she'd wrapped herself firmly, irrevocably around his heart. He couldn't imagine what he would have done had he not gotten here in time.

"You all right?" he asked.

She nodded, tears glistening in her eyes. "You saved my life. Again."

He grinned. "You owe me."

Her expression shifted from one of relief to one of worry. "Where's Maggie?"

"Paramedics have her."

"Is she…?"

He forced a reassuring smile. "She's strong. She's got a lot to live for. My money's on her coming out of this just fine."

Sophie's worry lines deepened. "Where's Ally?"

Gary swore under his breath, standing and then hoisting Sophie to her feet. "I gave her to the next-door neighbor. We'd better go."

"What about Trevor James?"

"Nowhere in sight, but you're safe now."

But Sophie gripped his elbow as he turned

to walk away. When he paused to face her, he saw something in her features he'd never seen there before.

Unchecked emotion. Raw and real.

"I'm so sorry," Sophie murmured. "If I'd left it alone, none of this would have happened. I should have listened to you."

Gary shook his head. "You followed your heart." He pressed a kiss to her forehead. "I can't fault you for that."

"But James got away."

"We'll find him." Determination bubbled to life inside him. "I'll find him."

A tear slipped over Sophie's lower lashes. "He's hurt so many lives."

Gary nodded. "We'll make him pay. Don't worry." He smiled, trying to ease the heartache painted across her face. "You'll get your man…and the story."

Sophie's expression grew more intent, more sad.

"Do you really believe I pursued this for the headline?"

Surprise skittered through Gary. Surprise and shame. He'd been lashing out when he'd made that comment, and he'd been completely off base.

"Well—" he chose his words carefully, wanting to assure her he thought no such thing "—you do have quite the reputation in the news community, but I was out of line. I know why you pursued this."

He met her gaze and his gut caught.

She was so beautiful. So driven. So strong. If only she'd see that and believe in herself.

"You did this out of love." He spoke the words softly.

Her features brightened instantly and fresh tears welled in her eyes. "Thank you."

He winked and squeezed her hand. "Don't take this the wrong way, but you won't be on-camera again anytime soon."

He tipped his head toward the house next door as fire personnel rushed past them. "Let's go."

A LINE OF NEIGHBORS formed behind the police tape as Gary rushed toward the house next door. He'd left Sophie with a medical worker, promising to find Ally and then let her know the child was safe.

Gary cast a second glance at the crowd as he raised his hand to knock on the neighbor's door.

That's when he saw him.

Trevor James.

Blending seamlessly into the gathered crowd of curious onlookers.

Their eyes met and James went into motion, moving quickly through the others, heading across the street, as if in defiance of the fact Gary stood between him and the person he sought.

Ally.

"Over here."

A woman's voice drew Gary's attention and he turned, shocked to see the neighbor he'd left Ally with standing outside, holding his niece in her arms.

James spotted the pair at the exact same moment and broke into a sprint, brows furrowed in determination.

"No!"

Gary screamed the word and the woman turned, frozen to the spot as James rushed toward her. Gary broke into a sprint, cutting a diagonal between James and the woman.

He ducked his head and lunged, his

shoulder connecting with James as the two of them slammed to the asphalt street.

James scrambled, struggling to free himself from Gary's grip, but Gary proved to be stronger. Slamming a fist into James's face, taking great satisfaction at the sound of the man's altered nose breaking beneath the blow.

"That's for my sister and my niece." He slammed his fist into the man's jaw. "And that's for Sophie."

The woman he loved.

The full realization hit him like a ton of bricks.

A handful of police officers rushed over to break up the fight. When one young man grasped Gary and pulled his arms behind his back, Gary tipped his head to where James now lay unconscious.

"That's the guy you want. He set the fire and he's responsible for at least three deaths that we know of."

Gary watched the reaction on a second officer's face as the man studied James's face.

"Isn't that Trevor James?"

The grouping of officers looked from Gary to James and back again.

Gary rubbed his fists and stretched his arms as the first cop released him.

"That," he said, "is his assumed identity. You're looking at a murderer and a crook named Kirk Johnson who's left a trail of destroyed lives from here to Bradston."

The officers frowned in unison.

"I don't follow you," one lone cop spoke out.

"Don't worry, you can read all about it in tomorrow's paper."

He tapped James's side with his toe. "You might want to check out the next issue of the *Inquirer*."

James's eyes blinked open, devoid of all reaction, as usual.

"I'm going to use my *simple reporting*," Gary continued, "to blow your cover sky-high."

As he walked away, headed toward where the paramedics were attending to Sophie, he felt more satisfaction than he'd felt in a long time. And when he met Sophie's gaze, he felt something so completely right, it took his breath away.

He felt love, and he saw his love returned in the blazing, unchecked emotion shining brightly in her eyes.

Forget the job in Los Angeles.

He had everything he needed right here at home.

SOPHIE WATCHED AS MAGGIE bundled Ally into her arms. Maggie had regained consciousness, much to everyone's relief, especially Ally's. The little girl had cried with joy when her mother's eyes had opened.

It was in that moment Sophie truly knew who Ally's mother was. Her mother was the woman who had rocked Ally on sleepless nights, who had bandaged her scraped knees, who had chased away her nightmares and encouraged her little-girl dreams.

And even though Sophie knew Becca would have given anything to be the mother doing all those things for Ally, Sophie was confident Becca would approve of the woman who was.

After all, a true mother would lay down her life to protect the child she loved, and Maggie had done just that, instinctively knowing what she'd had to do.

Just as Sophie knew exactly what *she* had to do now.

Epilogue

The children on the playground scampered from slide to swings, sandpit to teeter-totter. Sophie smiled, warmed from within at the sight of so many happy, carefree faces.

She could learn a lot from their uninhibited joy, their lack of concern about how they might look or what anyone might think.

As she watched, she reflected on the past several days.

Trevor James had been indicted for the murders of Becca, Teresa Cartwright and Brian Franklin. The police had found souvenirs from each of his crimes at the mansion he'd purchased thanks to his life-coach persona.

Among the items had been one of Becca's hairbrushes. A complete strand of hair had proved what Sophie had known from the day she'd first seen Ally.

Ally Alexander had been Robin Markham at birth.

Even though James had admitted to the adoption placement, it was nice to have solid proof.

But Sophie no longer needed that proof.

She'd lost her desire to remove the child from the Alexander home, even though she hadn't lost her desire to be part of Ally's life. She wanted the little girl to continue to know the love and security she'd known with Maggie and Robert.

Cook had been right. Ally was where she was supposed to be. She'd found her forever home, and with the love and support of her parents, she'd be able to move past the emotional scars caused by Trevor James's attack and deceit.

Speaking of Cook, he'd made a full recovery. But he'd decided not to come back to work right away. He and his beautiful bride had taken the trip he'd always put off. Two weeks in Hawaii.

Sophie smiled just thinking of the postcard

he'd sent. Blue skies and sunny beaches. Not a bad idea, when she thought about it.

Robert and Maggie had each made strong recoveries, even though Robert would require a few weeks of physical therapy to regain some motion in his arm. The doctors said he'd been lucky.

James, no doubt, had left him for dead, and if Gary and Sophie hadn't come along when they had, James might have gotten his wish.

"Hey."

Gary's voice sounded from behind Sophie and she turned, amazed—as she was every day—at the way the sight of him made her smile.

She knew she probably looked like a schoolgirl with a crush, but she didn't care. For once in her life, she was learning to feel, not think.

Gary had passed on the job in Los Angeles. He'd been hired away by a local news magazine after his exposé on Trevor James. His *simple reporting* had gotten his talents noticed. Big time.

As for Sophie, she'd taken an extended leave from work, wanting to let herself come to terms with everything that had happened. She'd made her peace with Becca's memory and had decided to forgive herself for not doing more, both during her sister's life and after her death.

"Ready?" Gary tipped his chin toward the picnic basket Sophie had packed. "I'll carry that."

He stooped to pick up the basket, stopping to brush a blade of grass from her high-tops. "Nice shoes."

She'd wanted to make a statement about the new-and-improved Sophie, and she remembered how much Gary had loved her sneakers back in college.

Gary's blond brows lifted and he grinned, the smile spreading wide across his face. "Welcome back."

Sophie frowned. "From where?"

Gary straightened, pressing his mouth to hers, kissing her deeply. When he broke away and took a backward step, he smiled again.

"From wherever it was you retreated to all of these years. It's nice to have you back."

He was right. She'd gone far away without going anywhere at all. She'd retreated, choosing a life with no emotional involvement over the risk of getting hurt.

He turned toward the park's open field.

"Gary." Sophie's heartbeat quickened at the thought of what she was about to tell him, what she was finally ready to tell him.

He paused, looking back at her, then frowning at the expression she knew she wore.

"My mother killed herself because she couldn't tolerate being alone. She went through one man after another, and in the end, they all left her."

Gary's features softened and he quickly closed the space between them, cupping her chin in his fingers. "You're not your mother."

"What if I am?" Her voice had gone so soft it was barely more than a whisper. "She was needy. Terribly needy."

Tears blurred her vision, and Gary put down the basket and enfolded her in his arms.

"You are anything but needy." His warm breath brushed against her hair and she relaxed into his touch. "You've been alone as long as I've known you, and you survived."

"But I was never happy."

An odd sort of relief eased through her with the admission.

Gary held her out at arm's length and grinned. "I've been thinking."

Sophie narrowed her gaze, waiting for whatever it was he had to say.

"Maybe you should give the alternative a try. Maybe instead of being alone, you'd reconsider that question I asked you back at school."

She inhaled deeply, giving him a watery smile, barely able to believe the depth of love she felt for the man before her. "How can you forgive me after what I put your family through?"

"You didn't put them through anything." He pulled her into his arms again. "Kirk Johnson put them through it. You just helped set things into motion." He pressed a kiss to her hair. "You're good at that, you know."

She laughed softly against his chest, then pushed away to look up at him. "Okay."

"Okay what?" He frowned.

"Ask me again." She tipped her chin toward him.

A hopeful smile spread wide across his face, and Gary dropped to one knee. "Marry me."

Emotion choked her, but Sophie forced her one-word answer through the lump that had formed in her throat.

"Yes." She reached for his hand, urging him to his feet.

When she kissed him this time, it was with abandon. "I love you," she whispered after their lips parted.

"I love you, too." Gary winked, bending once more to pick up the basket. "Come on, I'm starved."

But instead of heading for the open field, he took her hand and steered her toward the parking lot.

"Don't you want to—"

The hot desire in his gaze answered her question before she could finish asking it, and Sophie realized she'd never have to worry about Gary leaving. Never have to worry she'd made the wrong decision in giving him her heart.

In that moment, she understood how right their life together would be, and she silently acknowledged how secure and safe his presence made her feel.

All she'd ever needed—all she'd ever wanted—stood right before her, in Gary.

"Ready?" Gary's brows lifted.

Sophie nodded and reached out her hand, knowing she'd like nothing more than to follow him home.

* * * * *

Be sure to pick up Kathleen Long's next heart-stopping romantic suspense when RELUCTANT WITNESS debuts in December 2006, only from Harlequin Intrigue!

Set in darkness beyond the ordinary world.
Passionate tales of life and death.
With characters' lives ruled by laws the everyday
world can't begin to imagine.

Introducing NOCTURNE, *a spine-tingling*
new line from Silhouette Books.

The thrills and chills begin with
UNFORGIVEN
by Lindsay McKenna

Plucked from the depths of hell, former military
sharpshooter Reno Manchahi was hired by the gov-
ernment to kill a thief, but he had a mission of his
own. Descended from a family of shape-shifters,
Reno vowed to get the revenge he'd thirsted for all
these years. But his mission went awry when his
target turned out to be a powerful seductress, Mag-
dalena Calen Hernandez, who risked everything to
battle a potent evil. Suddenly, Reno had to transform
himself into a true hero and fight the enemy that
threatened them all. He had to become a Warrior for
the Light….

Turn the page for a sneak preview of
UNFORGIVEN by Lindsay McKenna.
On sale September 26,
wherever books are sold.

Chapter 1

One shot...one kill.

The sixteen-pound sledgehammer came down with such fierce power that the granite boulder shattered instantly. A spray of glittering mica exploded into the air and sparkled momentarily around the man who wielded the tool as if it were a weapon. Sweat ran in rivulets down Reno Manchahi's drawn, intense face. Naked from the waist up, the hot July sun beating down on his back, he hefted the sledgehammer skyward once more. Muscles in his thick forearms leaped and biceps bulged. Even his breath was focused on the boulder. In his mind's eye, he pictured Army General Robert Hampton's fleshy, arrogant fifty-year-old features on the rock's surface. Air exploded from between his lips as he brought the avenging hammer down. The boulder pulverized beneath his funneled hatred.

One shot...one kill...

Nostrils flaring, he inhaled the dank, humid heat and drew it deep into his massive lungs. Revenge allowed Reno to endure his imprisonment at a U.S. Navy brig near San Diego, California. Drops of sweat were flung in all directions as the crack of his sledge-hammer claimed a third stone victim. Mouth taut, Reno moved to the next boulder.

The other prisoners in the stone yard gave him a wide berth. They always did. They instinctively felt his simmering hatred, the palpable revenge in his cinnamon-colored eyes, was more than skin-deep.

And they whispered he was different.

Reno enjoyed being a loner for good reason. He came from a medicine family of shape-shifters. But even this secret power had not protected him—or his family. His wife, Ilona, and his three-year-old daughter, Sarah, were dead. Murdered by Army General Hampton in their former home on USMC base in Camp Pendleton, California. Bitterness thrummed through Reno as he savagely pushed the toe of his scarred leather boot against several smaller pieces of gray granite that were in his way.

The sun beat down upon Manchahi's naked shoulders, grown dark red over time, shouting his half-Apache heritage. With his straight black hair grazing his thick shoulders, copper skin and broad face with high cheekbones, everyone knew he was Indian. When he'd first arrived at the brig, some of the prisoners taunted him and called him Geronimo. Something strange happened to Reno during his fight with the name-calling prisoners. Leaning down after he'd won the scuffle, he'd snarled into each of their bloodied faces that if they were going to call him anything, they would call him *gan*, which was the Apache word for *devil*.

His attackers had been shocked by the wounds on their faces, the deep claw marks. Reno recalled doubling his fist as they'd attacked him en masse. In that split second, he'd gone into an altered state of consciousness. In times of danger, he transformed into a jaguar. A deep, growling sound had emitted from his throat as he defended himself in the three-against-one fracas. It all happened so fast that he thought he had imagined it. He'd seen his hands morph into a forearm and paw, claws extended. The slashes left on the three men's faces after the fight told him he'd begun to shape-shift. A fist made bruises and swelling; not four perfect, deep claw marks. Stunned and anxious, he hid the knowledge of what else he was from these prisoners. Reno's only defense was to make all the prisoners so damned scared of him and remain a loner.

Alone. Yeah, he was alone, all right. The steel hammer swept downward with hellish ferocity. As the granite groaned in protest, Reno shut his eyes for just a moment. Sweat dripped off his nose and square chin.

Straightening, he wiped his furrowed, wet brow and looked into the pale blue sky. What got his attention was the startling cry of a red-tailed hawk as it flew over the brig yard. Squinting, he watched the bird. Reno could make out the rust-colored tail on the hawk. As a kid growing up on the Apache reservation in Arizona, Reno knew that all animals that appeared before him were messengers.

Brother, what message do you bring me?

Reno knew one had to ask in order to receive. Allowing the sledgehammer to drop to his side, he concentrated on the hawk who wheeled in tightening circles above him.

Freedom! the hawk cried in return.

Reno shook his head, his black hair moving against his broad, thickset shoulders. *Freedom? No way, Brother. No way.* Figuring that he was making up the hawk's shrill message, Reno turned away. Back to his rocks. Back to picturing Hampton's smug face.

Freedom!

Look for UNFORGIVEN
by Lindsay McKenna,
the spine-tingling launch title from
Silhouette Nocturne™.
Available September 26,
wherever books are sold.

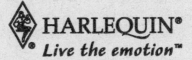

...there's more to the story!

Superromance.
A *big* satisfying read about unforgettable characters. Each month we offer *six* very different stories that range from family drama to adventure and mystery, from highly emotional stories to romantic comedies—and much more! Stories about people you'll believe in and care about. Stories too compelling to put down....

Our authors are among today's *best* romance writers. You'll find familiar names and talented newcomers. Many of them are award winners— and you'll see why!

If you want the biggest and best in romance fiction, you'll get it from Superromance!

Emotional, Exciting, Unexpected...

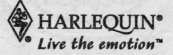

HARLEQUIN®
Live the emotion™

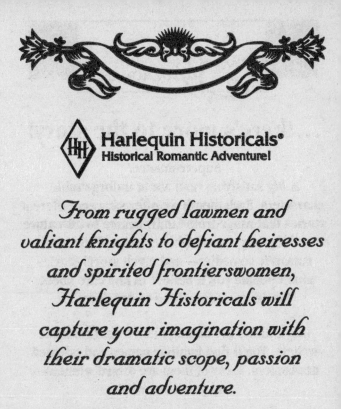

Harlequin Historicals®
Historical Romantic Adventure!

From rugged lawmen and valiant knights to defiant heiresses and spirited frontierswomen, Harlequin Historicals will capture your imagination with their dramatic scope, passion and adventure.

*Harlequin Historicals...
they're too good to miss!*

SILHOUETTE *Romance*

Escape to a place where a kiss is still a kiss...

Feel the breathless connection...

*Fall in love as though it were
the very first time...*

Experience the power of love!

Come to where favorite authors—such as

Diana Palmer, Stella Bagwell, Marie Ferrarella

*and many more—deliver modern fairy tale
romances and genuine emotion,
time after time after time....*

*Silhouette Romance—
from today to forever.*

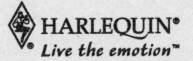